Dare to Be Rare

kwm
kathleen whitten
MINISTRIES

Some ways the world tells me that "I am not good enough" are:
"Just walking down the halls of school you feel inferior, not cool, good, pretty, or smart enough." (12th grader); "The way I look . . . I am always self-conscious about my weight." (12th grader); "How much money you have and if you are perfect or not." (8th grader); "People not liking me back" (12th grader); "It's hard to think of what I am good at." (10th grader)

To me, "Dare to Be Rare" means:
"Living outside my comfort zone and declaring my love for God through actions no matter what others think." (12th grader); "Be myself and not conform to the pattern of this world. I am beautiful just the way I am." (12th grader); "Go against the crowd when you know what they are doing is wrong and don't be afraid to stick up for what you believe in." (8th grader)

Because of Dare to Be Rare, I dare to:
"Fix a lot of things in my life that I know I've needed to but haven't had the strength and courage to do." (12th grader); "Stop trying to impress people and just be who God wants me to be." (10th grader); "Live life now—don't worry about what others think. Be you—all of you!" (9th grader); "Not give up!" (12th grader)

Some things Kathleen said about herself and her life that meant a lot to me are:
"We can all relate . . . her struggles through junior high and high school. . . ." (10th grader); "You just blew my mind away . . . ! It made me feel like I was really beautiful on the inside. And you made me know that I should just be myself because God made me that way and (we all) like you for that. Thank you for speaking to ME!" (6th grader)

I want to tell Kathleen:
"That DTBR was a wonderful idea because it helps girls to love themselves for who they really are." (9th grader); "You have been through so much and I look up to you because you turned to God every time." (10th grader); "That you make me open my eyes and see things about Jesus that I never would have seen." (10th grader); Can you speak to us again?" (9th grader)

Praise for Dare to Be Rare

"In *Dare to Be Rare*, Kathleen Whitten shares with us both our purpose for living and the way to live with purpose. She breaks open the Word and exposes all of our fears and excuses until finally we are ready to eagerly embrace the amazing inheritance that is ours."

—Terry Meeuwsen, co-host, *The 700 Club*

"*Dare to Be Rare* is a guide through the maze of young adulthood. Always challenging; always hopeful; filled with stories that will make you smile and marvel at God's immense love. Kathleen's love for Jesus is on every page."

—Chuck Collins, Rector, Christ Church, San Antonio, Texas

"Our creator is the master affirmer. He gives purpose and direction to our lives. Kathleen Whitten's *Dare to Be Rare* encourages women to live a life of purity and purpose. An excellent book."

—Linda Strom, speaker and author of
Karla Faye Tucker Set Free: Life and Faith on Death Row

"*Dare to Be Rare* reveals Jesus in such a way that you know He's in the seat next to you, holding you tight as you travel the ups and downs of life's roller coaster. Kathleen will love you, challenge you, and lead you to discover the joy of living with Christ by your side."

—Cheryl Marting, Chief Connections Officer, Auxano, Houston, Texas

"*Dare to Be Rare* is a life-changing book, journal, small group tool, parent/youth leader resource . . . and movement. Through her books, ministry, and conferences, Kathleen Whitten is leading a whole generation of women and girls to turn their eyes to God's Word, their hearts to His love, and their lives to His plan."

—Mike Bickle, International House of Prayer of Kansas City

"*Dare to Be Rare* arms young girls with information they can use in helping them grow to adulthood with their strength and purpose intact. The loss of self-worth and value in our young women today is alarming. We need to get this book into the hands of our daughters, granddaughters, nieces, and friends so they can understand that God made them special and unique and learn to love the person God made them to be."

—Rich Marshall, author of *God @ Work Volume I* and *Volume II*

"This is a wonderful book, with something special to offer readers of every age. No matter what challenges in life you are facing, it will reward you with new insights with each reading. I loved it!"

—Dr. Denise Woody-Gross,
gynecologist specializing in female needs, San Antonio, Texas

"Kathleen has been an amazing spiritual mentor to me since high school. Her encouragement and guidance to me has always been based on God's word, which she continues to do throughout this book. Kathleen's realness about her trials and triumphs have greatly blessed my life. Michael and I are so excited for all of the lives she will bless through her teachings in *Dare to Be Rare!*"

—Ginna & Michael Crocker, Reverend,
Alamo Heights United Methodist Church

"Today's teenagers need truth and relevant, personal application. Kathleen Whitten weaves many personal examples with God's truths to hit the bull's eye of a young person's heart. Every young person that you work with would benefit by these quick-hitting, personal topics of *Dare to Be Rare!*"

—LeRoy Jacobson, San Antonio Youth for
Christ/Campus Life, in youth ministry for 36 years

"*Dare to Be Rare* will help a young person discover her belovedness, so that she can live her life in the freedom of who she is in God's grand design. I wish I had had access to her words of wisdom and encouragement when I was a young girl."

—Bitsy Ayres Rubsamen, spiritual director, retreat speaker,
prayer minister, and author of *Gentle Rain* and *Becoming the Beloved*

"As a pediatrician who has been practicing for 39 years, I see this as a valuable resource for girls of all ages, especially preteen and teenagers. It gives them scriptural references and applications to help them make wise decisions during these important years."

—J. Thomas Fitch, M.D., Pediatrician, San Antonio, Texas,
past President of the Texas Pediatric Society,
Focus on the Family Physicians Resource Council,
Chairman of the Board of the Medical Institute for Sexual Health

Dare to Be Rare

A Christian Guide for Girls

Kathleen Whitten

MOREHOUSE PUBLISHING
An imprint of Church Publishing Incorporated
Harrisburg – New York

Unless otherwise indicated, Scripture taken from the HOLY BIBLE, NEW INTERNATIONAL VERSION®. Copyright © 1973, 1978, 1984 International Bible Society. Used by permission of Zondervan. All rights reserved.

Scriptures marked (NKJV) are taken from the New King James Version. Copyright © 1982 by Thomas Nelson, Inc. Used by permission. All rights reserved.

Scripture quotations marked (KVJ) are taken from the Holy Bible, King James Version.

Scripture quotations marked (AMP) are taken from the Amplified® Bible, Copyright © 1954, 1958, 1962, 1964, 1965, 1987 by The Lockman Foundation. Used by permission. (www.Lockman.org)

Morehouse Publishing, 4775 Linglestown Road, Harrisburg, PA 17105

Morehouse Publishing, 445 Fifth Avenue, New York, NY 10016

Morehouse Publishing is an imprint of Church Publishing Incorporated.

Cover photography by Weiqin Bao

Cover design by Laurie Klein Westhafer

Journaling and reflection questions by Lauri Hahn

Library of Congress Cataloging-in-Publication Data

Whitten, Kathleen.
  Dare to be rare : a Christian guide for girls / Kathleen Whitten.
    p. cm.
  ISBN 978-0-8192-2283-1 (pbk.)
  1. Teenage girls—Religious life. 2. Teenage girls—Conduct of life. 3. Christian women—Religious life. 4. Christian women—Conduct of life. I. Title.
BV4551.3.W45 2007
248.8'33—dc22
                              2007029490

Printed in the United States of America

07 08 09 10 11 12   10 9 8 7 6 5 4 3 2 1

kathleen whitten
MINISTRIES

To my husband, Lacey, whose pure, unselfish love gives me the grace to
DARE TO BE RARE.

"Do not be conformed to this world, but be transformed
by the renewing of your mind that you may prove the will of God,
that which is good, acceptable, and perfect." (Romans 12:2)

Contents

Acknowledgments

My Heavenly Father, Who gave me life.
Jesus, Who gives me mercy and eternal life.
The Holy Spirit, Who continually offers guidance, peace, and miracles.

My precious children, Mattie and Storm, you are my heart.
Mom, Dad, Katha, Leslie, and Meg, who loved me first.
The Whitten family who loved me second.

Lauri Hahn, whose invaluable support made this book possible.
The *kathleen whitten ministries* **Prayer Team**, who daily prays through it all.

The "Wednesday Group," Sunday Application Class," Christi Moorman, and all the amazing men, women, and teenagers in my life who encourage and inspire me to discover and share with them—the rare treasures in God's Word.

Introduction

Most of us start out thinking we're pretty special. I remember visiting my daughter's prekindergarten class.

"Who's the best artist?" I asked. Every hand in the room went up.

"Who's a good friend?" Again, every hand flew up.

"Who is really, really smart?"

"Me," they shouted, "ME!"

Little kids also seem to have enough confidence to make friends instantly. Their conversations begin something like this:

"What's your favorite color?"

"Blue."

"I like blue."

"Yeah."

"Do you wanna play?"

"Yeah."

"Okay, you get on the merry-go-round. I'll push."

When my daughter was about four, I bought her a new dress. She put the dress on right away and then stood in front of the mirror and began twirling in a circle happily.

"Oh Mommy," she said, "I look prettier than I even am!"

We start out happy with ourselves. So what happens? What happens to us between ages five and ten (or fifteen, or eighteen, or twenty-five, or forty-five)?

What happens to the little girl who used to like herself? What happens to the little girl who used to draw pictures and sell them to the neighbors? What happens to the little girl who sang and danced confidently in front of all the relatives?

What happens to the little girl who would lie down in the backyard on a summer night and count the stars—and be glad she is who she is?

I can tell you what happens.

Slowly

Over time

The world

Tells her

That she is not so special

That she is not so pretty

That she is not so talented

That she is not much . . .

And she believes it.

I want you to hear my heart right now. I want you to understand this is a lie that you might believe—completely or even just a little bit.

The lie: "You cannot be *you* to be loved. If you want to be loved and accepted, then you have to change to be someone else."

The truth: God made you to be *you!* And you will only be truly happy when you stop trying to be somebody else.

How do I know?

Because for years I believed I wasn't enough. I wasn't pretty enough. I wasn't smart enough. I wasn't fun enough. I wasn't cool enough. I believed that I wasn't enough because through the years people—knowingly and unknowingly—had rejected the real me.

I learned to not like the way I looked. I learned to not like the way I talked. I learned that some girls seemed more important and more worthy of love and attention from others. And I learned to change to be more like them—and as I did that, I learned to not like the real me.

And along the way, I lost the real me, and deep down inside I became empty.

Many days my heart was anxious. Who will I sit with at lunch? What if people laugh at me or ignore me or just leave me out?

Many days my heart broke a little as I watched some girls laugh at others and say mean things about them—and then act happy. (Are they really happy?) And I watched as other girls walked down the hall alone, year after year. (Does anyone know their names?)

Day after day I saw these things. Day after day I realized something wasn't right.

At that time in my life there was no one else to turn to. So I cried out to the Jesus of my childhood.

And He heard.

He wrapped His arms around me.

He wiped away my tears.

I can't tell you how exactly, but Jesus began healing me and gave me something that answered the questions and the cries of my heart. Jesus gave me Words that would forever change my life:

"Do not be conformed to this world,
but be transformed
by the renewing of your mind,
so that you may prove what the will of God is,
that which is good and acceptable and perfect." (Rom 12:2, NASB)

In other words: *Dare to Be Rare*

I carried that Scripture passage on a crumpled piece of paper in my pocket in high school and prayed every day that I would be the real me God wanted me to be, and that I would also allow others to be their real selves.

1. This book is for young people, who need to know just how special they are to God.
2. It's for anyone needing to know that God has a purpose for their lives.
3. It's an excellent guide for those who are desiring to follow Jesus.
4. And for one who is searching, asking, wondering—it's a treasury of truth.

You can use this book in lots of different ways. Maybe you received it on a youth retreat, and you're reading it with other people your age. Or maybe you're reading it on your own. If you are, here are some suggestions for getting the most out of this book:

- Find a quiet place and set aside some time to read, pray, and reflect. It might be in your room at bedtime, or during study hall, or in the car on a long trip with your parents. Find out what works best for you.
- Read one chapter a day, and spend some time thinking about what you've read and how it applies in your life.
- Spend a few minutes in prayer. You can pray the prayer at the end of each chapter, or you can talk to God in your own words.
- Write down your thoughts and feelings. You can jot down notes in the margins of this book, or you can buy a notebook and start a prayer journal.

There are lots of ways to use this book. Find the way that works best for you.

Many years have passed since Jesus gave me that Scripture passage, but my heart still burns with the same passion—to *Dare to Be Rare!*

You're not reading this by chance. Those who have put this book together are praying that people who God wants to have this book . . . will. That's you. . . . God is calling you now to not conform. Jesus is telling you now he created you precious and special and unique.

Now is your time to *DTBR*.

Prologue

I call these devotions "shish-ka-bobs."

They came about when I couldn't find any devotions for small groups. Christians wanted *meat* not *milk*, but most of the devotionals that were *meat* were *steaks*—too long to devour and for many, too big to swallow.

God gave me a little idea for SHISH-KA-BOBS—*meat* you can take with you. Meat you can digest. Meat that will give nourishment for a generation on the run.

May the Holy Spirit speak to you personally as He will!

kathleen whitten

One

Hey, Where Are You Going with That?

Giving God Your Burdens

Growing up, there were times when one of my little sisters would take something breakable or valuable of mine and wander off.

Sometimes I would catch her in the act and say, "Hey, where are you going with that? That doesn't belong to you. Give it back!" Then she would try to run away and hide.

Do you think God ever feels the way we do when someone takes His stuff? Does He ever say, "Hey, where are you going with that? That doesn't belong to you. Give it back!"

Think about this: Any situation important to us is valuable to God. Any situation worrying us could be considered breakable. And if we are His, our worries or burdens are His as well.

Do we, as Christians, ever carry off something breakable or valuable that belongs to God and wander aimlessly holding it in our hands?

Ask yourself: When I hear of a problem within my family, what do I do? When I learn of a struggle a friend is going through, what do I do? When situations arise that I don't know how to handle, what do I do?

Many Christians tend to take those burdens in their own hands and wander off with them. Sometimes we go to our rooms and bury them. We even run from God when He tries to take them!

Galatians 6:2 says to "bear one another's burdens." The word "bear" in the Greek (the original language of the New Testament) is *bastazo* (bas-tad'-zo), meaning "to carry, or take up."

Some people think this means they're responsible for everyone's problems and worries. But that's not what God intended.

As Christians, we are to pick up or bear the problems of others as it says in Galatians 6:2. But what we do with this burden after we pick it up is the key.

The Bible clearly says we should pick up the burden, go to God, and give it to Him. Jesus says:

> "Come to Me, all you who labor and are heavy-laden and overburdened, and I will cause you to rest. (I will ease and relieve and refresh your souls.) Take My yoke upon you and learn of Me, for I am gentle (meek) and humble (lowly) in heart, and you will find rest (relief and ease and refreshment and recreation and blessed quiet) for your souls. For My yoke is wholesome (useful, good—not harsh, hard, sharp, or pressing, but comfortable, gracious, and pleasant), and My burden is light and easy to be borne." (Matt 11:28–30, AMP)

Christ tells us in this Scripture passage to carry our burdens to God and leave them with Him. When we do this, God will take our yoke and give us His yoke.

Do you know what a "yoke" is? In this passage, the Greek word for yoke is *zugos* (dzoo-gos'). *Zugos* (yoke) has two meanings: Farmers, especially those who lived in Jesus' day, knew what a yoke is. It's a wooden instrument placed on the neck or back of oxen or cattle as a hitch so that these beasts of burden can plow the field or pull a heavy load. A yoke makes it possible for animals to do all the farmers' work. But the word yoke has a spiritual meaning, too. It can mean any burden we might carry on our backs, or any burden we carry as our responsibility. Cleaning our rooms might be our yoke, or helping a friend who's sad or angry.

But Jesus tells us not to hang on to those yokes. He says that we should carry our yokes over to Him and place them in His hands—our worries, our sins, our breakable problems. In return, He promises, He will give us back a yoke that's light and easy.

Think about This

What is that light and easy yoke we are to always carry with us? *Christ's love and the faith that God is at work on our problems so we don't have to be.*

Just like my little sister, we are *not* to run away with God's breakables—whether they're our burdens or someone else's—or hide them away. We need to give those burdens back to the owner—God.

The next time you hear prayer requests and problems from friends or family or anyone you happen to meet, what will you do? What will you do the next time you feel sad, worried, or overwhelmed?

If you pick up all the problems and begin to wander around with them, you just might hear God say to your heart, "Hey, where are you going with that? That doesn't belong to you. Give it back!"

Lay every problem and every burden at the feet of Jesus for Him to take care of. Not only will Jesus work on the situation, but He will make your heart light as you trust in Him.

Pray

Lord, You tell us in Galatians 6:2 to bear or carry each other's burdens. But You tell us in Matthew 11:28–30 to give You those burdens (yokes) so You can give us the light and easy yoke of trust and love.

Jesus, I choose to take every care and burden to You right now: me, my family, my friends, health, future, finances, spirituality, decisions, dreams, my past, my future, today—everything!

I choose to trust You to take care of those breakable, delicate, valuable situations and people in my life, and work everything out for good according to Your excellent plan for me.

Teach me that even when I hear of huge problems or when I need big miracles, I should pick up that situation, in prayer, and take it to You.

Please forgive me for worrying and carrying a heavy yoke upon my back. I take Your light and easy yoke now because I have decided to trust You with every burden. Amen.

Believe

"Come to Me, all you who labor and are heavy-laden and overburdened, and I will cause you to rest. (I will ease and relieve and refresh your souls.) Take My yoke upon you and learn of Me, for I am gentle (meek) and humble (lowly) in heart, and you will find rest (relief and ease and refreshment and recreation and blessed quiet) for your souls. For My yoke is wholesome (useful, good—not harsh, hard, sharp, or pressing, but comfortable, gracious, and pleasant), and My burden is light and easy to be borne" (Matt 11:28–30, AMP).

For Journaling and Reflection

1. Remember this: God is way bigger than any problem you'll ever have. So instead of letting your worries overwhelm you, ask God to remind you of five things that are going well in your life. Write them down, and then ask Him to help you think about your problems in a new way. After a few days, try to notice if you're thinking a little differently about your problems. Write down any changes you notice.

2. Have you ever watched a best friend or family member worry about something that you just *knew* was going to work out? That's how God feels watching you worry. You can't see the outcome, but He can. What are you carrying around that's weighing you down, distracting, or exhausting you?

3. Fill in the blanks: "I feel like I can handle everything that's going on in my life, except_____." Now, imagine what your days would be like if you didn't have to worry about it. Say a prayer asking God to carry that burden for you, along with all the rest of your worries.

4. Have you ever gone to sleep worrying about something, then woken up in the morning and, for a moment, completely forgotten about it? How did that feel? When you let go of your cares, God takes them. How would it feel to be that free of your worries all day long?

Two

Light Reflectors
Being a Light in a Dark World

I went to one of those giant sports stores recently to buy some tennis shoes. The salesperson held up a pair of running shoes he thought might work for me and said, "Do you ever walk in the dark?"

I asked him, "Why? Are those shoes fluorescent so they glow in the dark?"

"No," he said, "they aren't fluorescent, because they don't glow on their own. They're called 'light reflectors.' The light from cars and street lamps will reflect on the shoes so people can see you in the dark."

This made me think. What the salesperson said reminded me of Matthew 5:14, which says, "You are the light of the world. . . ."

As Christians, we are to be the *light* in a world that keeps getting darker and darker. But how can we constantly shine in dark places?

Being a light to a dark world can be challenging—if not impossible—if you think you have to be fluorescent—always glowing in the dark on your own.

Why? Ask yourself these questions:

+ If I'm in a group of people who don't love or respect God (or themselves, or anyone)—how can I be a light?
+ If I'm tired and even sad or hopeless about something—how can I be a light?
+ If I'm exhausted or burned out—how can I shine for everyone else?
+ If I don't have the answers to a big problem and I'm really worried about it—how can I be a light to an already dark world?

So if you realize that *you* can't be a light to the world—how can Matthew 5:14 be true? That's easy: Because God never intended for us to be the light—He wants us to reflect His Light.

Think about This

God wants us to be His light reflectors.
He is the source of light!

We're not the source of light. Our good works aren't the source of light. Our obedience isn't the source of light. Our understanding, or wisdom, or intelligence aren't the source of light either. God is the only source of light. An awesome example of a light reflector in the Old Testament is Moses: "The LORD would speak to Moses face to face, as a man speaks with his friend. Then Moses would return to the camp" (Exod 33:11). After speaking with God—the source of light—Moses' face would reflect the light of God so strongly that the people were actually afraid: "So when Aaron and all the children of Israel saw Moses, behold, the skin of his face shone, and they were afraid to come near him" (Exod 34:30, NKJV).

The word "shone" in this passage in Hebrew is *nrq qaran* (kaw-ran'). The word has lots of meanings, but the most important one is "to send out rays."

The Hebrew word *shone* means reflected!

As a matter of fact, Moses' face reflected God so strongly, and the people were so afraid, that Moses had to wear a veil to cover it. Now that's a light reflector: "And till Moses had done speaking with them, he put a veil on his face" (Exod 34:33, KJV).

Think about This

When Jesus died on the cross, the temple veil dividing the Holy of Holies (the place where God resided, where only the high priest could enter) was supernaturally torn in two, letting everyone see God's glory for themselves. Because of Jesus, we can now reflect the glory of God completely unveiled for all to see.

A good example in the New Testament of a light reflector is John the Baptist: The Bible says in John 1:7 (NKJV) that John came to "bear witness of the Light (Jesus), that all men through Him (Jesus) might believe." John 1:8–9 (KJV) goes on to say, "He (John) was not that Light, but was sent to bear witness of that Light. That was the true Light, which lighteth every man that cometh into the world."

Jesus is the source of light. Like John the Baptist, our job is simply to reflect the Light—Jesus—and His Word. We need to be human light reflectors!

When you look into a mirror, you see a reflection of the original you. A light reflector is kind of like that. It simply mirrors the light that's been shone on it. The light is all about the source of light—God. It's not about the reflector—us.

"When Jesus spoke again to the people, he said, 'I am the Light of the world. Whoever follows Me will never walk in darkness, but will have the light of life'" (John 8:12). Do you know what that means? That means Jesus is the original—and only—source of light. He's the only source of truth, love, hope, goodness, and if we reflect him—if we mirror, follow, copy, and learn from Him—we don't have to walk in the darkness of depression, despair, confusion, evil, or fear.

So what do I need to do to become a light reflector? Here's a three-step guide:

1. **Get near the Source.** Remember my light-reflector sneakers? They only "shine" when a headlight—a light source—shines near them. So draw near to God. God promises us

that when we draw near to Him, He'll draw near to us (Jas 4:8). Talk to God. He always hears and understands, so God "the Source" will be near us. His light will shine on us—His reflectors.

2. **Ask God to put you with other light reflectors.** Can you imagine jogging in the dark with a group of people wearing light-reflective gear? A glowing example! Get with a group of light reflectors—the brighter the better. Share with each other ways to get near to the source: prayer, reading the Bible, going to church, and worshiping are some good examples. Go to God and ask Him to illuminate your path to show you which group of friends is the best one for you.

3. **Put on your reflective gear.** My reflective tennis shoes won't do me any good in the closet. If I'm outside in the dark and want some light reflection, then I have to put them on. We live in a "dark" world. There are things all around us that are dark and evil. We need to make sure we are always light reflectors, because there are so many temptations in the dark.

Sometimes there's a temptation to do or say the wrong thing. And sometimes, even if God gives us the grace to do or say the right thing, there's a temptation to believe the evil around us is so big, peer pressure is so strong, people are so dishonest, addictions are so powerful, and the world is so corrupt, that our little reflective light doesn't matter. But that's not true.

Get this picture: The darker the room, the brighter the light. If I shine a flashlight in a well-lit room, then it hardly shows up. But if I shine it in a pitch-black room? Wow! That's what the writer is talking about in the letter to the Romans: "But where sin increased, grace increased all the more" (5:20).

That means that no matter what dark situation you find yourself in, God will increase His grace to meet all your needs. No matter how bad things get "down here" on earth—God will increase His light to overcome darkness.

The darker the room—the brighter the light!

Pray

Dear Jesus, I want to reflect Your love and truth in my life. Thank You for not expecting me to be a source of light but only a reflector. Help me to learn that if I try to be my own source of light—my own source of strength, love, wisdom—then sooner or later I'll just burn out.

God, I believe You are the original and only source of light. Only You are my source of truth, love, hope, goodness, and if I reflect you—if I mirror, follow, copy, and learn from You—then I don't have to walk in darkness. You'll protect me from the darkness of depression, despair, confusion, evil, or fear.

Help me to get near Your Light through the Holy Spirit, Your Truth, Your Word, and Your people so I can reflect You more and more strongly in a world that grows darker and darker.

Psalm 23 and Isaiah 58:8 say that even during my darkest hour I will see Your light through the darkness and shadows because Your light will always be behind me, protecting me. Amen.

> "Even though I walk through the valley of the shadow of death, I will fear no evil, for You are with me; Your rod and Your staff, they comfort me." (Ps 23:4)
>
> "Then your light will break forth like the dawn, and your healing will quickly appear; then your righteousness will go before you, and the glory of the LORD will be your rear guard." (Isa 58:8)

Believe

"When Jesus spoke again to the people, He said, 'I am the Light of the world. Whoever follows Me will never walk in darkness, but will have the light of life'" (John 8:12).

"You are the light of the world" (Matt 5:14).

Always remember this: You are God's light reflector.

For Journaling and Reflection

1. Was there ever a situation where you could have reflected God's light, but the darkness felt too deep and being a light reflector just felt impossible? Looking back, what could you have done differently? Try to imagine how things might have turned out if you had reflected God's light. In your notebook or journal—or in the margins of this book—write about the way that incident happened. Then write about how it might have happened if you'd been a light reflector for God. Write down a prayer asking God to help you let others see God's bright light shining through you.

2. Is there a particular situation, group, or place where it always seems hard to reflect God's light? Why? What can you do to help you make different choices?

3. We all find ourselves in situations ranging from dimly lit to pitch dark, but even when we can hardly see in front of us, God gives us ways to find His light. Maybe you have a gift for listening to a friend who's sad, or maybe you can help organize a plan when everybody else is worried and confused. Those are gifts from God that you can use to help reflect His light in dark moments. What are some special ways that you can reflect God's light? Write down some of your gifts and think about ways you can turn them into light reflectors.

4. Do you have a group of light-reflecting friends? Are there people you can think of whose shining company you can share regularly? Are there some darker situations where you're the one called to reflect God's light?

Three

Mirroring Honor
When Honoring Your Parents Is Difficult

Not long ago, I told my mother I needed to look for a large mirror for my dining room wall. She said she had two mirrors at her house, and I could have one. After several days of measuring and thinking and even changing my mind, I finally chose the one I liked—a small, simple gold one.

Both Mom and Dad said they were glad my husband and I could use it, and we were so thrilled to finally have our carefully chosen mirror. But soon after that, my parents came over for dinner. When they saw the mirror on my wall, my father thought the whole situation over some more, and while I was out of the room, he told my mother that I couldn't keep the mirror after all. Instead, Dad insisted I draw for which mirror would be mine. He felt this was better than letting me pick one, since I have two sisters who might someday need a mirror, too.

Mom reluctantly went upstairs and told me about my Dad's change of heart and asked me to draw a piece of paper with a number on it. There were three mirrors, she explained: the two that I had seen at her house and a huge, gaudy one at our family's ranch. Each number referred to one of those mirrors.

I asked her what we would do if I drew the huge, giant gaudy mirror. "Don't worry," she said, "you have a two-thirds chance of drawing one of the two mirrors you've already seen and liked." Tired, and a bit irritated by the change of plans, I chose one of the numbered pieces of paper and showed it to Mom. "Which mirror is number one?" I asked. Mom rolled her eyes and halfway grinned. Well, it was a cross between a grin and a grimace.

"You drew the big mirror from the ranch," Mom said, "and I need to tell you something. There's a family legend surrounding that mirror. Your

11

great-grandparents bought it in a Colorado saloon years ago and told your grandparents—who told us—that there's a valuable painting of a nude behind the mirror."

Silence. Great, I thought. There goes my elegant gold mirror, replaced by a huge one that's too big for our room, complete with an obnoxious old-time painting of a naked woman with high lace-up boots, lying on a red velvet couch.

So much for taste. So much for *fair*. A lot of things went through my mind. Things like *redrawing*. Things like *forgetting* to swap out the mirrors. A lot of things.

Mom said it was hard for her make me draw, even though Dad suddenly made it mandatory, because I'd worked so hard at picking between the two at her house, and she had already given one to me.

Why did Dad have to step in and change things around? This is unfair!

I began praying about it. I was hurt. I was frustrated. I was confused about what to do or not do. But one of the Ten Commandments kept coming back to me: "Honor thy father and thy mother" (Exod 20:12, KJV).

Why didn't the Bible go on to say, "except when a parent is really flaky and changes his mind after he's already promised"? Instead this same Scripture passage kept repeating in my heart: "Honor thy father and thy mother."

"Honor" in the Hebrew language is the word *kabad* (kaw-bad') or *kabed* (kaw-bade'). The most common translations of the word are "to honor, to glorify, and to make weighty."

What does it mean to make someone or something weighty? That sounds like an odd definition for honor, but it isn't. Think about it: If you give a lot of weight to something, then you give it value. If I put a lot of weight in what you say, then I am honoring your words or acknowledging that they're important. God is commanding us to give a lot of weight—honor—to our parents. And to give weight to what they say is the opposite of blowing them off or making light of them.

> "Honor thy father and thy mother" (Exod 20:12).

Here's the clincher: Even if you think your parents are wrong—even if you think you *know* they're wrong—you still need to honor what they say if you want to be blessed.

And if you grab your Bible and look up the Ten Commandments, you'll see that "honor your mother and father" is the only one of the commandments with a personal blessing attached to it. The blessing is if we honor (place weight upon what our parents say) then, our "days may be long upon the land which the LORD thy God giveth thee" (Exod 20:12, KJV). Translation: Honor your parents, and you'll have a good long life.

As I look back, I can vividly remember times of honoring my parents (painfully—I might add) even when their decisions seemed like they were coming from the wrong motives. During my senior year in high school, I wanted to apply to a prestigious college out of state where I felt reasonably certain I would be accepted. But my parents didn't even allow me to apply, because they felt that the school was too far away and didn't share our family's values. So much for making good grades—I thought at the time. So much for freedom of choice.

A few weeks after I made my college choice—from the narrow list my parents approved—I met a young man at a party. To make a long story short, that young man is now my husband. Honoring my parents brought me an unexpected blessing: Lacey and I were able to date and really get to know each other during my first years of college and his three years at law school, since we were just a short car trip apart.

. . . .

Think about This

God always has a plan. And He always blesses us for honoring our parents, even if what they ask of us seems unfair.

. . . .

Back to the mirror story. As God so often orchestrates things, my husband, my daughter, and I already had plans to go to the ranch with some friends. When we got there, I took one look at that big baroque mirror and almost forgot about the whole "honor your mother and father" thing. The mirror looked so huge, ornate, and heavy on the simple ranch wall, but since I'd already decided to honor my father's wishes, I knew I had to lug the heavy thing home.

Why does it seem that the right thing to do is sometimes the heaviest and hardest? It took the strength of two men to move that mirror into our car. It was raining and slippery and a mess outside. When we got the mirror home, we placed it against the buffet table in the dining room and saw at once that it would look beautiful hanging on the dining room wall.

Isn't it strange? Sometimes when a situation or thing looks really bad, but you move it to a different location or even a different light, it suddenly appears completely different.

The next day I called a friend of mine. She's an artist who restores old paintings, I told her about the family legend of an oil painting behind the mirror. She said that after all that time the painting would probably stick to the back of the mirror and need a lot of work to fix up. But she was willing to help me take a look.

A few days later, she and her mother—also an artist—came over to see if there was a way to unveil the mysterious painting without damaging it. Again we needed two men to lift the mirror. Amazingly, there were two painters taking a break outside my door. They promptly laid the heavy piece upside down on a thick comforter on top of my dining room table. Slowly, the two restorative artists removed protective paper from the back of the mirror along with old screws and the hanging chain. Finally, the two women were ready to lift the old linen canvas from its four-generation resting place behind the mirror.

I had the only perfect view as the canvas was lifted and laid as gently as a baby onto another blanket. At first I couldn't say a word. The oil painting turned out to be a beautiful pastel in perfect condition. It is a tastefully drawn nude of a woman from behind. The word that most people utter after seeing it is "exquisite," and since I know so little about art, I agree and repeat, "Yes, exquisite indeed."

The handwritten date next to the artist's signature is 1901. This beautiful pastel had been hidden behind a mirror for one hundred years! Isn't it interesting that God planned the timing so that the pastel would be revealed in 2001, exactly one hundred years after it was created?

If I hadn't done things God's way, I would have kept the small mirror I'd chosen in the first place. But because I honored my father and mother (which I wish I could say was always the case), I received a beautiful family heirloom pastel and a gorgeous mirror and, most importantly, the satisfaction of knowing that God picked both of them out just for me.

What did I learn from this? Probably more than I can write. First, as a daughter, I learned I don't have to agree with my father and mother, but I have to honor—and place much weight—on what they say. And if my mother hadn't honored my father, even though she felt he was being unfair, then I wouldn't have had the opportunity to receive the blessing.

As a mother, I want to give my children the opportunity to receive God's blessing in all circumstances. But if I remove the opportunity for them to obey or do the hard thing, then I rob them of the opportunity to receive the blessing as well.

Now as a wife, I want to honor my husband and place weight on what he says even if I might not understand or agree—just as he does for me. Honoring your spouse isn't always easy. There have even been times when my husband and I have honored one another's wishes even though our children and even friends and family might not have understood, appreciated, or agreed. But God has shown me the protection and blessing He gives me in a strong marriage where my husband and I love and respect each other.

We need to ask God to help us honor Him, our parents, and our spouses no matter how difficult it may be. There is always a blessing in mirroring honor.

Think about This

One note: If a parent or a spouse ever demands something of you that goes against the law of God or the law of the state, please seek help from a school authority, church, or someone you trust. God never asks us to do something that is contrary to His Word.

Pray

Jesus, please teach me to honor my parents and what they say. Sometimes this seems unfair and very difficult, but I trust that when I honor them, there will always be a blessing for me. I trust that even if I believe they are wrong, You will work it out for my good because I have honored them.

Forgive me for the times I have put little value in what my parents have said. Forgive me for the times I have not honored them. Please give me the grace to do the right thing so I may receive blessings in my life. Amen.

Believe

"Honor your father and your mother, that your days may be long upon the land which the Lord your God has given you" (Exod 20:12).

For Journaling and Reflection

1. Think of a time when you went against your parents' wishes and you ended up regretting the way things turned out. How did you feel? How can you prepare yourself for the next time you need to honor your parents' wishes rather than doing things your way?
2. Write down a few reasons why you think God chose your specific parents for you. In what ways do they understand you better than anyone else? In what ways does that make things easier? In what ways does that make things harder?
3. Why do you think God chose this commandment over the others to be followed with a blessing? Why might the parent-child relationship be so valuable to God the Father (hint: look up John 3:16 and Matthew 3:17), and how does Jesus demonstrate honoring a parent's wishes (John 12:49 and Matthew 26:42)?

Four

In the Meantime

Surviving the Dry Seasons of Life

In Texas, we have an expression that goes like this: "If you don't like the weather, just wait a while and it will change." For the most part, that's true. But Texas summers can have extremely long stretches of hot, dry weather that seem to never end.

During these scorching times, our water is rationed, our yards turn brown, and everyone seems cranky except companies that sell and repair air conditioning. By midsummer we are yearning for cooler weather, a break from the oppressive heat, even a little rain.

But most South Texans know the key to staying peaceful during the heat is staying cool. And staying cool can't depend on the weather to change, because it likely will not. Staying cool depends on what you do in the meantime.

If we focus on the soaring temperatures, talk about how hot we are, and complain about our plants dying, then it will be a long, hot season. But if we water our yards the best we can, sip some lemonade in the shade, and take a cool dip in a swimming pool whenever possible, summer will seem to fly by.

The seasons of our lives are a lot like that. Some seasons can be long, hot, and even oppressive. It's tempting to decide that our peace and joy will return as soon as the season changes, but seasons can last a while— even years.

So what do we do in the meantime? First of all, realize there is a *meantime*.

I was speaking to a friend on the phone who was waiting for her eye to heal completely. She said she trusted God but waiting in the meantime

17

was the hardest part. We both agreed that the meantime can feel like mean time. Prisoners even call their jail sentences doing time.

Probably the hardest time for any human being is the meantime: The time in between where you are and where you want to be. And guess what? Although God gives us great joys and many blessings, we will be spending a lifetime on this earth going through one meantime after another.

The meantime is the time between your question and your answer. The meantime is the season it takes to heal. The meantime is the time you might feel lonely or unappreciated, or the time you are in an unpleasant situation. The meantime is the time when everything seems to be going wrong. The meantime is the season when you are calling out to God . . . but don't seem to hear an answer.

Our life on this earth is even meantime—the time between where we are and where we are going to be—Heaven.

A man in the Bible, Job, certainly experienced some meantime. Everything was taken away from him. His family was killed, his money and property were gone, and his body was wracked with pain. In his grief and agony Job says, "May the day perish on which I was born" (Job 3:3, NKJV).

Have you ever felt that way? Like everything is going so badly you wish you had never been born?

To make things worse, Job and his friends make the meantime even meaner because their minds are completely occupied with figuring out *why* all these terrible things are happening. Job then spends a lot of time feeling shameful and asking God, "Why me?"

God never does explain to Job *why*. But after Job admits to God he doesn't have answers and needs all the help from God he can get (Job 42:3–6), God goes to work to restore all that Job lost. Job 42:12 says the Lord blessed the latter days of Job more than his beginning and increased all that he had.

Truly, God promises us He will bless us, His children, more in our latter days (our eternity with Him in heaven) than our former days (our time on this earth). But He also gives us restoration, and healing, and miracles, and answers here on this earth. God likes solving our *meantimes*, and He is the only One Who can.

Are you in the meantime right now in a certain situation? What should you do? What do any of us do in the hot, dry season? What do we do when the heat is so oppressive we cannot breathe?

Just like Texas summers, yearning for a change in season doesn't make our long hot summers cooler any more than yearning for our situations to change makes them better. The only answer is what we do in the meantime.

Think about This

When you encounter a long, oppressive, hot season in your life what can you do in the meantime?

Dive into God's Word. The Word is refreshing and good. It takes the heat off all situations. When I was diagnosed with cancer, there were certain Scripture passages I thought about all day long and even said out loud—all during the meantime. One of my favorites is Proverbs 4:20–22: "My son, pay attention to what I say; listen closely to my words. Do not let them out of your sight, keep them within your heart; for they are life to those who find them and health to a man's whole body."

Write down simple Scripture passages that speak to you and hold onto them. There are so many promises in the Bible. Find one and focus on it instead of your difficult situation. (And don't hesitate to ask your parents, pastor, or friends for help in finding Scripture passages that pertain to your situation.)

Admit to God He is the only One with the answers. Learn from Job and his friends that trying to figure out what God is doing or who is at fault makes the meantime meaner. Acknowledge to God that you are depending on Him to get you through.

Realize the season will change. Truly, if you hold on and trust God, it may be sooner than you think. When I lost all my hair to chemotherapy, it felt like I would be bald forever. When I was in labor with my child, it seemed like it would last forever. When I was in a body cast for a year as a teenager following back surgery, I thought I would never get out.

Even today, I'm facing a giant meantime. And I would be surprised if you weren't also.

Let's trust God together. Let's have peace in every season—even in the meantime. God loves us so much. He is waiting with miracles, and restoration, and love, and joy, and healing, and blessing beyond our imaginations.

Pray

Dear Jesus, You know the things I am going through—no one else can understand. I admit it is completely up to You to help me. Please show me what to do, heal me, guide me, and in the meantime please keep me in Your peace. Amen.

Believe

"My son, pay attention to what I say; listen closely to my words. Do not let them out of your sight, keep them within your heart; for they are life to those who find them and health to a man's whole body" (Prov 4:20–22).

Choose a verse that means something to you and write it down in a place where you can look at it again and again.

For Journaling and Reflection

1. What was the last "meantime" you went through? Are you going through one now? How are you getting through it? What changes can you make to help you depend on God to get through it?

2. What season is your life in right now? Spring: new beginnings? Summer: carefree, relief of pressures? Fall: shifting gears, getting down to business? Winter: rest, barrenness, waiting? Look back over some of the other seasons in your life. What have you learned in each of those seasons? As you think about them, think about ways that God was at work in your life even when it seemed like nothing much was happening.

Five

Someone Is Watching

God Sees It All

Have you ever been aware of someone doing something wrong and not getting caught? Maybe this person appears to be honest or nice, but you know about some things they did that aren't so honest and nice—and you seem to be the only one who knows.

Maybe you've seen people get away with cheating or lying, or maybe they've even hurt you in some way. Maybe they stole something or tricked somebody or misled someone into believing a lie.

Maybe you see someone in your school or your town do bad things every day, and it burns you up that they get away with it. Or maybe you see a national figure—even an authority figure—misbehaving, and you wish that everyone in the country would open their eyes to the truth.

Have you ever wondered, "Is anyone watching?"

On the flip side, have you ever noticed someone who does good things and never gets noticed? Have you been aware of a person who is treated unfairly? Do you know someone who is never appreciated for the good things he or she does? What about a behind-the-scenes person who never gets credit for their hard work or kindness?

Have you ever questioned, "Is anyone watching?"

Well, I have exciting news for you. It's good news, but it's a little bit scary, too.

Someone *is* watching.

His name is God, and there isn't one thing that gets past Him.

People who cheat, lie, betray, and hurt others may think they're getting away with it. But they're sadly mistaken. God sees it all. And someday those who continually do evil without asking for forgiveness will stand before God and answer for all the things they've done.

Matthew 6:4 is one of the many Bible verses that tells us Our Heavenly Father "sees what is done in secret." He sees it all.

The bad news: We all have things we've said or done in secret that we know are wrong.

The good news: When we confess those things to God and sincerely ask for forgiveness through Jesus, then those ugly things are wiped off our slate for good.

Think about This

When we confess our sins and ask for forgiveness, God says He will not remember those bad secrets, and our reputation with God will be clean.

Repent means to turn the other way. When we turn away from our sins and turn to God, then He forgives and forgets. Here are some Scripture passages that tell us about God's amazing forgiveness:

> "For I will forgive their wickedness and will remember their sins no more." (Jer 31:34)
>
> "For I will forgive their wickedness and will remember their sins no more." (Heb 8:12)
>
> "Then he adds: 'Their sins and lawless acts I will remember no more.'" (Heb 10:17)

Always remember: When we confess our mistakes to God, ask for forgiveness, and then repent, God makes Himself forget them.

How else could King David pray this prayer in Psalm 25:7: "Remember not the sins of my youth and my rebellious ways; according to Your love remember me, for You are good, O LORD."

This is incredible news: When we ask for forgiveness and repent, then God promises to forget we ever did something wrong. Don't you wish everyone would forgive and forget like God does?

But what about the good things we do? What about the good things that have been done in secret and no one has noticed or appreciated? What does God do with those?

God makes Himself forget the bad things we've done after we've asked for forgiveness—even when *we* remember them. But He promises to always remember all the good things we've ever done, even when we forget them.

God not only sees all the good things done in secret, but He remembers them always and He rewards them. Here's what the Bible says, "[God,] Who sees what is done in secret, will reward you" (Matt 6:4, 6)

As a matter of fact, the Bible says it's better when God is the only One who has seen you do these good secret things:

> Be careful not to do your "acts of righteousness" before men, to be seen by them. If you do, you will have no reward from your Father in heaven. So when you give to the needy, do not announce it with trumpets, as the hypocrites do in the synagogues and on the streets, to be honored by men. I tell you the truth, they have received their reward in full. But when you give to the needy, do not let your left hand know what your right hand is doing, so that your giving may be in secret. Then your Father, who sees what is done in secret, will reward you. And when you pray, do not be like the hypocrites, for they love to pray standing in the synagogues and on the street corners to be seen by men. I tell you the truth, they have received their reward in full. But when you pray, go into your room, close the door and pray to your Father, who is unseen. Then your Father, who sees what is done in secret, will reward you. (Matt 6:1–6)

What does God mean by reward? The word "reward" in Matthew 6:6 is translated from the Greek word *apodidomi*. *Apodidomi* (ap-od-eed'-o-mee) means "to pay, give, or render." It suggests paying what is due or giving back (restoring) what is owed.

That means God will pay us somehow or in some way even when those who might owe us never do.

So what could a reward be? A reward from God could be any awesome good blessing that God chooses. Maybe you secretly sent a valentine to someone who you knew would never receive one otherwise. God never forgets the good you do even after you forget. So ten years later, when you're feeling down and you least expect it, someone mysteriously sends you a special card and a dozen roses. Or maybe, out of the blue, somebody says a kind word or gives you a compliment that cheers you up in the middle of a really bad day. God's rewards are greater than we can imagine. They can be financial, providing for our needs when things look really bleak, or they can be emotional, giving us joy when our lives seem to be filled with sorrow. They can be relational, providing loyal friends, great boyfriends, and later spouses and children, or they can be physical, such as fitness, healing, and freedom from pain. But God's rewards are always spiritual, too, and they're always better than we could even ask for. The Bible explains it this way:

> "Now to Him who is able to do immeasurably more than all we ask or imagine, according to His power that is at work within us, to Him be glory in the church and in Christ Jesus throughout all generations, for ever and ever! Amen." (Eph 3:20–21)

So when we do the things God asks us to do, He promises to reward us in many ways. But listen—He also promises to never forget the good things we have done. Hebrews 6:10 says God "will not forget your work and the love you have shown Him as you have helped his people and continue to help them."

Let's read this passage in the book of Hebrews:

> God is not unjust; He will not forget your work and the love you have shown Him as you have helped His people and continue to help them. We want each of you to show this same diligence to the very end, in order to make your hope sure. We do not want you to become lazy, but to imitate those who through faith and patience inherit what has been promised. When God made His promise to Abraham, since there was no one greater for Him to swear by, He swore by Himself, saying, "I will surely bless you and give you many descendants." And so after waiting patiently, Abraham received what was promised. (Heb 6:10–15)

In other words, hold on. Keep doing good and believing God will bless you 'cause it ain't over 'til it's over.

To sum it up: If you're doing the things you know God wants you to do and no one seems to notice—if you are doing special and good things for people in the name of Jesus and in secret, God promises He will never forget it, and He will reward you. So hold on, and keep doing those good things, even if no one else in the world seems to care.

But if you're doing things you know you shouldn't be doing and think you are getting away with it, then you are *very wrong*. Take the time now and admit to God what He already knows. He has so much love for you that He promises to wipe your record clean when you repent and ask for forgiveness.

Pray

Lord Jesus, the more I read of Your Word, the more I see of Your goodness. Your plan and Your way of doing things is almost too good to be true. But I know it's true because You never lie.

First of all, Lord, I need to admit _____. Please forgive me in the name of Jesus and wash me clean of guilt and shame. Please help me not to _____. Please help me to forgive myself and accept the fact You have forgiven me, and You have chosen to forget that I have ever done this wrong thing. Please give me Your grace in order to do what is right and to stop doing what is wrong. I can't do it without You.

Lord, in the areas where I am (with Your grace) trying to do what is right, please help me to continue doing the right thing even when no one on this earth notices or cares. Thank You for seeing and remembering the good that I do in secret. I believe my reward is from You, and I trust You to always have the perfect blessings for me. Amen.

Think about This

If there's a repetitive sin in your life that you hate and you can't seem to stop yourself, or if there's something bad you've done that you can't seem to receive forgiveness for, don't hesitate to get help. God wants you to be free of that thing so you can live a prosperous, joyful, and full life. Get help to quit. Talk to your parents, your pastor, or your teacher. Do not let the devil fool or shame you into accepting a life of slavery to any addiction or evil thing.

"No temptation has seized you except what is common to man. And God is faithful; He will not let you be tempted beyond what you can bear. But when you are tempted, He will also provide a way out so that you can stand up under it." (1 Cor 10:13)

Believe

God forgets:

When you repent of sin and ask God for forgiveness, God says in Jeremiah 31:34, "For I will forgive their wickedness and will remember their sins no more." (Also: Heb 8:12, 10:17.)

God remembers:

When you do good things in secret according to God's will, Hebrews 6:10 says, "God is not unjust; He will not forget your work and the love you have shown Him as you have helped His people and continue to help them."

For Journaling and Reflection

1. Have you ever been in the middle of a very rough day when suddenly, something wonderful happened that turned everything around? God was watching—and so were you. Write a note to the person who made that day better, expressing your appreciation. Tell that person how God blessed you with their kindness—and say a big thank you.

2. Is there a hidden sin in your life that you know God wants you to give up? Why do you feel like it's worth hanging on to?

3. Think of three people you can bless without them knowing it was you. Carry those blessings out and then don't tell anyone else about it.

4. What happens when you're tempted to believe that God could never help you out of your particular mess? Does it make you want to give up on yourself? On God? Challenge yourself to trust God to forgive you and to help you forgive yourself.

5. God promises to always give you a way out of a tempting situation. What are some of the harder temptations for you? Write a prayer asking God to give you wisdom and strength to recognize (and take) His way out of your next temptation.

Six

Is Purpose a Bad Word?
Following God's Plan for Your Life

My six-year-old daughter asked me a strange question: "Is purpose a bad word?"

A little surprised, I questioned her, "What makes you think the word purpose is bad?"

"Well," she said, twirling in a circle as only six-year-olds can do, "sometimes when I'm about to get in trouble, you ask me if I did it on purpose."

"No, no, honey." I tried not to grin. "Doing things on purpose isn't always a bad thing. Purpose can be a very good word. We try to do 'good things' on purpose—even when it's hard—like listening to Mommy and Daddy, or being nice even when someone is mean, or doing what God wants us to do even when we don't want to. If we don't do these good things on purpose, then we probably won't do them by accident, and we'll probably get in trouble."

"Oh," she responded, falling dizzily onto the floor.

As I walked out of her room, God began to show me what I had just told her applies to all of us as Christians. Like my daughter, we can begin to think of purpose as only a negative word. And we can focus so much on what we are purposely not going to do that we miss out on what we purposely should be doing. For example, you might focus so much on not acting impatient with your mom that you forget to compliment her for fixing your favorite meal.

The Apostle Paul is one man who did everything he did *on* purpose and *with* a purpose. When Paul believed that Jesus was an impostor and an enemy of God, he tried to destroy Jesus' followers—on purpose. But when God got hold of Paul and showed him that Jesus was truly

His Son, then Paul set out to tell the world the good news of salvation through Jesus Christ—on purpose.

You've probably heard God has a special purpose for each of us. Part of fulfilling our purposes in God comes from doing things God's way on purpose.

A strong sense of purpose—and making up our minds to follow God's purpose—is a very big deal. I believe God used Paul in such mighty ways—and even allowed Paul to write two-thirds of the New Testament—because Paul was so purpose-driven.

In the New Testament, the word we translate as purpose comes from the Greek word *protiyemai* (prot-ith'-em-ahee), which means "to place before or to set forth." So the word "purpose" means to set before one's self, propose to one's self, to purpose, and to determine. So if I'm to live my purpose in God, I have to set before myself His Word, propose to myself that with His grace I will follow it, purpose within myself to do it even when I don't want to, and determine I will (with all His help) fulfill His awesome plan for me. Practically speaking, I have to purposely put a high priority on learning what God says through the Bible and then purposely make the decisions that will keep me in God's good plan for my life. For example, God says that my body is the temple of the Holy Spirit. So I need to *purposely* take care of my body by eating healthily, exercising, and staying away from drugs because I will have many temptations and opportunities to not do the right thing.

Of course, God is so good that He gives us grace to help us, miracles to encourage us, angels to lift us up when we fall, people to minister to us, the Holy Spirit to guide us, His Truth to protect us, His Word to feed us, and the list goes on.

But deciding to do the right thing on purpose is up to you.

And no one can decide that for you . . . no one.

Choosing to follow God on purpose doesn't determine whether or not we go to Heaven, because we receive salvation through believing, asking, and receiving: We believe that Jesus is God's Son. We ask for forgiveness for our sins. And we receive Jesus as our Savior.

But if we do the believing, asking, and receiving and leave out the determining to follow God on purpose, then we will end up detouring our whole lives. Sure, we'll go to Heaven, but our lives here on this earth will be a frustrating mess.

Have you ever been on your way to a certain destination and half the streets were under construction? After taking detour after detour, you didn't even know where you were anymore, and you were so turned around and frustrated you wanted to give up.

That's what the devil wants you to feel about your Christian walk on this earth—frustrated, off God's path, taking detours, upset, late, worried, and even wondering if you were on the right road to begin with. Get the picture?

Now, a little note for those of us who have detoured more than we would like to admit: Romans 8:28 says, "And we know that in all things God works for the good of those who love Him and who have been called according to His purpose."

So when you love God, and He has called you to be His—that's what he wants for all His children—then even your detours will work out for good.

Isn't that just like God—to give us incredible blessings in our detour? Doesn't that make you love Him more?

So what is our purpose? Thankfully, God makes it simple. In Exodus 9:16 He says, "But I have raised you up for this very purpose, that I might show you My power and that My name might be proclaimed in all the earth."

Think about This

God raised us when He raised Jesus. He saved us. He loves us. And He created us to declare His name in all the earth. Now that's purpose!

God shows us His power every day: through the creation and birth of a baby, through miracles, through nature—through all that He has created! And this Scripture passage says that He raised us up not only to see His power, but to declare His name.

Now, you may be a little word weary, but I am a word fanatic. So let's look at the word "declare."

"Declare" in this verse in Exodus comes from the Hebrew word *caphar* (saw-far), and it means "to write, to tell, to number, to count, to show forth, to recount, to relate, to reckon, and to talk."

So our job is to write, tell, show, and talk so that the Name of God is glorified in all the earth.

To do this, we have to determine to declare His name on purpose, because there are plenty of times when we wouldn't want to do it. But God gives us the strength and grace to overcome our weaknesses so we can fulfill our purpose every day.

Think about This

How do I tap into this power to help me fulfill my daily purpose?

1. **Depend on God to help you.** The psalmist wrote these earnest appeals for help and depended on God to fulfill his plan and purpose:

    "I cry out to God Most High, to God, Who fulfills His purpose for me" (Ps 57:2); "The LORD will fulfill His purpose for me; Your love, O LORD, endures forever—do not abandon the works of Your hands" (Ps 138:8).

2. **Realize every day is a choice to reject or embrace God's purpose.** Luke 7:30 tells us "the Pharisees and experts in the law rejected God's purpose for themselves."

    You can reject God's purpose for your life (not to mention your day). We need to humbly seek God to guide us and help us.

3. **Have a humble heart.** Listen to this humble attitude from the purpose-driven Apostle Paul:

    I became a servant of this gospel by the gift of God's grace given me through the working of His power. Although I am less than the least of all God's people, this grace was given me: to preach to the Gentiles the unsearchable riches of Christ, and to make plain to everyone the administration of this mystery, which for ages past was kept hidden in God, who created all things. His intent was that now, through the church, the manifold wisdom of God should be made known to the rulers and authorities in the heavenly realms, according to His eternal purpose which He accomplished in Christ Jesus our Lord. (Eph 3:7–11)

No wonder God helped Paul all the time.

4. **Believe God has the power to accomplish His whole purpose in you.** Never forget that God "works in you to will and act according to His good purpose" (Phil 2:13).

Pray

Pray for yourself: God, thank You for working Your good purpose within me. I determine right now to do Your will on purpose even when my flesh doesn't want to. I know I will need all of Your help to do this.

Please forgive me for the many days I have not made it my purpose to glorify You and follow Your good plan. Thank You that even when I fail and take a detour, You promise that because I love You and am called according to Your purpose, You will work it all out for my good.

Pray for others: 2 Thessalonians 1:11 is a fabulous prayer to pray for your family, your friends, your Bible study, anyone God puts upon your heart to pray for: "With this in mind, we constantly pray for _____, that our God may count _____ worthy of His calling, and that by His power He may fulfill every good purpose of (his/hers/theirs) and every act prompted by (his/hers/theirs) faith." Amen.

Believe

In Exodus 9:16 He says, "But I have raised you up for this very purpose, that I might show you My power and that My name might be proclaimed in all the earth."

For Journaling and Reflection

1. Have you ever focused so hard on the bad things that *might* have happened that you missed a chance to do something good? Think about one of those times, and ask God to help you focus on the good things in the future.
2. How does doing things God's way on purpose (even when you don't feel like it) affect His special plan for your life? In what ways can it make your life harder to not purposely follow God's plan?
3. In what ways do you think you may have detoured from God's plan in your life? In what ways has God taken that detour and used it for good?

Seven

If Your Heart . . .

Confidence Before God

"Kathleen," a friend told me on the phone, "I feel I can never meet God's expectations."

My friend admitted she had a fear of never meeting God's expectations. Maybe that's your fear today. Maybe you're wondering what God expects of you—and if He's disappointed that you're not living up to it. But how can you think you're not meeting God's expectations if you don't really know what they are?

What does God expect of you and me—and all His children today and every day? Can you answer that question?

If you aren't sure of the answer, then why let the devil give you the answer? Satan would like to feed you lies like these:

God expects you to perform every good deed all the time as Jesus would. God expects you to be, act, and say everything perfectly and in perfect timing and in a perfect way. God expects no mistakes from you—especially if you've already apologized for the same mistake. God expects an hour of quiet time in the morning, cookies baked for the elderly in the neighborhood, hymns hummed at noon, complete memorization of of the Bible, and two solid hours on your knees in prayer before you fall into your bed. And then God expects you to start all over again the next day. God sees that you're not performing well, and frankly, . . . He is not happy. I would steer clear of God, if you know what I mean. Maybe slink around for a while and hope He doesn't notice you.

News flash #1: The devil is a liar!

News flash #2: God's expectations are very clear.

Check out these Bible passages:

> "And this is His [God's] command: to believe in the name of His Son, Jesus Christ, and to love one another as He commanded us" (1 John 3:23). "Love the Lord your God with all your heart and with all your soul and with all your mind. This is the first and greatest commandment. And the second is like it: 'Love your neighbor as yourself.'" (Matthew 22:37–39)

So here it is: God expects His children to love and believe Him and love each other.

So answer this: Most of us would say we love God, but do we you *believe* God?

Maybe you answered yes, you *do* believe God, but you're doing some things you know you shouldn't be doing. Well, that's an issue between you and God, but it doesn't change God's love for you because His love is not based on what you do. He loves you simply because you are His child.

So don't slink around and hope God doesn't notice you—that's the serpent's job. You're simply to believe God, and ask Him to help you get your life together, and *then* believe He will do it!

Jesus says, "Everything is possible for him who believes" (Mark 9:23).

Perhaps our prayer needs to be the very next verse of Mark: "I do believe; help me overcome my unbelief!" (Mark 9:24).

Even if you love God, if you don't believe what God says, that's a big deal to Him. God has taken great measures not only to prove His Word, but to make it possible for us to expect Him to always follow through on His promises.

God gave us the Bible filled with true stories about ordinary, imperfect people whose lives show us that God fulfills His every promise and loves His imperfect children. All God wants is for His children to love Him and believe Him—and to love one another.

And God will go to extremes to get His children to quit talking disbelief.

Example: Remember Zechariah? God promised Him a son even though he and his wife, Elizabeth, were *very* old.

When Zechariah was chosen to go into the temple and burn incense, the angel of the Lord, Gabriel, appeared to Zechariah and told him he and his wife would have a son named John (Luke 1:8–13). Gabriel explained that John would be a powerfully spiritual man who would "turn the hearts of the fathers to their children and the disobedient to the wisdom of the righteous—to make ready a people prepared for the Lord" (1:17).

Instead of saying, "Amen!" or "Thank you, Lord!"—as we hope *we'd* do if an angel appeared to *us*—Zechariah started talking disbelief. "How can I be sure of this? I am an old man and my wife is well along in years" (Luke 1:18).

Zechariah gets quite a reply from God's angel: "I am Gabriel. I stand in the presence of God, and I have been sent to speak to you and to tell you this good news. And now you will be silent and not able to speak until the day this happens, because you did not believe my words, which will come true at their proper time" (1:19–20).

And that's exactly what happened. Zechariah couldn't mutter a word for nine months. He couldn't speak until that baby was born. Why? Because Zechariah would have been talking against God's plan. He was speaking unbelief.

Whether you speak belief or unbelief is important because our words are very powerful indeed. God Himself says that our words have power for life or death, belief or unbelief. Proverbs 18:21 (NKJV) says, "Death and life are in the power of the tongue, and those who love it will eat its fruit."

Jesus tells the disciples in Mark 11:23, "I tell you the truth, if anyone says to this mountain, 'Go, throw yourself into the sea,' and does not doubt in his heart but believes that what he says will happen, it will be done for him."

And in Mark 11:24, Jesus makes a huge claim: "Therefore I tell you, whatever you ask for in prayer, believe that you have received it, and it will be yours."

Listen to this connection between belief and talking belief:

> The word is near you; it is in your mouth and in your heart, that is, the word of faith we are proclaiming: That if you confess with your mouth, "Jesus is Lord," and believe in your heart that God raised Him from the dead, you will be saved. For it is with your heart that you believe and are justified, and it is with your mouth that you confess and are saved. (Romans 10:8–10)

Conclusion: Don't let anyone convince you that what comes out of your mouth doesn't matter. Your mouth helps direct your life like a rudder directs a small boat. And God needed Zechariah's mouth to line up with the truth to head his life in the right direction. Zechariah was speaking disbelief, so God shut his mouth—that's an extremely powerful message.

Here's one more Scripture to chew on:

> The good man brings good things out of the good stored up in his heart, and the evil man brings evil things out of the evil stored up in his heart. For out of the overflow of his heart his mouth speaks. (Luke 6:45)

What is your heart overflowing with today? God asks you to believe Him and to trust He will bring all His words to pass in your life.

Are you speaking belief or unbelief today?

A wise Christian woman once told me, "Honey, when you speak the Word, then you never lie." You might be in a position today, she meant, that looks like your needs may not be met—maybe you're having relationship problems, or your car is breaking down, or things just seem out of whack.

If you say, "This is an impossible mess. I'll never get out of this one." Then you are talking unbelief.

But on days like that, turn to Philippians 4:19: "My God will meet all of your needs according to His glorious riches in Christ Jesus." Even through things are looking bad say, "God will cover my needs. He will care for me because I am His child. He makes the impossible possible." God is asking us to speak out of our mouths what we believe in our hearts to cooperate with His awesome plan.

When my youngest sister was little, she hated getting up in the morning. One Christmas morning, Mom went in her room to wake her up to tell her that Santa had been at our house.

I'm not sure exactly what her words were, but a loose translation is: "Get out of here and leave me alone."

Mom reentered her room a few minutes later and said, "Sweetheart, there's lots of gifts for you downstairs."

This time, my little sister responded with a sleepy, grumpy, "Nuh-uh."

Not to be thwarted, Mom persisted, "Believe me, you have a lot of wonderful things waiting. Come open your presents."

Soon after, my little sister did get up—and what a sight to behold! There were gifts and laughter and the cheer of the season. But if my little sister had had her way in the beginning, or if she'd chosen to not believe Mom and continue to say, "Nuh-uh," she would have missed out on many big blessings.

We too can talk ourselves out of God's gifts, blessings, and promises.

Listen: God does everything for His children because He loves them. He shut Zechariah's mouth so that Zechariah could not speak disbelief and mess up God's good plan.

What promises has God made to you in His Word that you still haven't seen fulfilled? What promises has He made to you personally? It's so important to God that we believe Him and speak belief.

If we feel as if we have been praying to a closed heaven, or don't have direction in a difficult situation, it could be that maybe—just maybe—

God knows He can't reveal His wonderful plan to us yet because we would speak disbelief just like Zechariah.

Decide to believe God:

+ That means believe God in the face of any obstacle—like Jonathan and Caleb. (Numbers 14)
+ Believe God when people all around you are going a different way—like Noah. (Genesis 6:5–8:16)
+ Believe God when your reputation is on the line—like Mary. (Luke 1:34–38)
+ Believe God even when it hurts so badly you don't think you can stand it . . . and you feel like you are sweating blood—like Jesus. (Luke 22:44)
+ That means believe God when His word and His plan say one thing even if every government, every specialist, every media network, every friend, every relative, every computer, every medical test, every committee, and everyone you can think of says the opposite of what God says: Still believe God.

That's it. It's that simple: God expects us to love and believe in Him and love one another.

We talked about the believing God part, but what about the loving others part?

Do you love God's other children?

Maybe your answer is "Yes, but . . ." Well, you're not alone. There are many, many people who most everyone would consider to be difficult or even impossible to love. But if you are a Christian, you have the power within you—the Holy Spirit—to love them anyway. So there's no excuse.

Do you think my words are too harsh? Do you think I have no idea what you've been through? Well, you're right—I don't. But God does. And God is both merciful and miraculous. If you choose to follow Him, then He'll give you the miraculous ability to forgive even those who have hurt you to the very core of your being. And understand this: Your complete healing comes only when you let go of the debt owed to you that no human can repay. Let go so that God can heal and restore you. Only He can repay you for your troubles. Believe Him and He will. Be patient.

> And on the morrow when he departed, he took out two pence, and gave them to the host, and said unto him, Take care of him; and whatsoever thou spendest more, when I come again, I will repay thee. (Luke 10:35, KJV)
>
> Dearly beloved, avenge not yourselves, but rather give place unto wrath: for it is written, Vengeance is Mine; I will repay, saith the Lord. (Rom 12:19, KJV)

When I was working with children who had been abused and removed permanently from their homes, I met a girl whose life had been especially difficult. Her mother had tried to murder her—she has a giant slash scar on her neck to prove it—and her father also abused her very, very badly.

She told me how hard it was to forgive her parents, who were both in prison.

This isn't pleasant reading, but I want you to understand that God's Word comes without, "Yes, but . . ."

I expressed to this special, hurting girl week after week that although she loved God and had asked Jesus to come into her heart and be her Lord and Savior, she still had to forgive her parents. Doesn't that sound harsh? Doesn't that sound uncompromising? Psychologists say it is really impossible under such severe and grotesque circumstances. But it's not impossible to God.

The next time we met, this girl ran up to me laugh-talking! Laugh-talking is my favorite way of communication—this girl was so full of joy she could hardly speak. She told me what had happened. She prayed in her bunk, "God, I can't forgive my parents, but You say that I have to—so I ask You to make it possible for me. I now choose to forgive Mom and Dad."

And between her laughter and her tears she explained that the Lord appeared to her. (Now, I'm not exactly sure what an eleven-year-old meant by "appeared," but suffice it to say that for her, God showed up.)

She said Jesus gave her this "wave of love" for her parents, and then He said He would heal the scars on her body and in her heart, but He would allow her to remember this great forgiveness so she would never do those things to her children.

Imagine: These were the words of an eleven-year-old orphan who has no one but a powerful Heavenly Father Who loves her and gave her the power to do what He asked her to do.

What unforgiveness do you have? If you haven't forgiven someone, then you cannot fully love them, and God expects us to love one another.

Pray and ask God to show you someone you don't love, then ask Him to help you love that person anyway. It doesn't mean that you become vulnerable or careless with your heart, but it does mean that between you and God and them, somehow peace has been made. God may also work a miracle in the process.

One girl was mean to me all through junior high and high school. In junior high she poured salt in my hair and told the boys that it was lice. In high school she had a way of embarrassing me in front of everyone and letting me and other girls know that I was not included in the crowd.

To the best of my ability, I was nice back to her, but I still had resentment and unforgiveness in my heart. Every time I saw her I got a knot in my stomach. I knew the beginnings of bitterness were not the feelings God wanted. So I asked Him to help me love and forgive her in spite of how she would probably continue to behave. I also began to pray for her every day.

Drastic changes took place in my heart as I genuinely began to care about her. However, I did not put my heart out to her to become a "door mat." When I saw her, I greeted her warmly (not expecting a response from her), but never called her on the phone or tried to be her good friend. I knew what she was capable of doing. So I avoided her as much as possible.

A few years later when I was crowned homecoming queen, she walked across one end of the football field to speak with me and said, "I voted for you."

I was dumbstruck.

She continued, "When we were in sixth grade I was so mean to you, but you weren't mean back. My parents and family were going through some difficult things when I was in high school, and I took it out on you. But you still only reciprocated in kindness. I just wanted you to know that I voted for you. You deserve it."

That is something that happened to me. But everybody has a special situation, with its own troubles and hurts. Only you know *yours*. Only you can go to Your Heavenly Father and ask Him how to make things right in your heart. But I promise: He will.

Now here is the best news of all:

> This then is how we know that we belong to the truth, and how we set our hearts at rest in His presence whenever our hearts condemn us. For God is greater than our hearts, and He knows everything. Dear friends, if our hearts do not condemn us, we have confidence before God and receive from Him anything we ask, because we obey His commands and do what pleases Him. And this is His command: to believe in the name of His Son, Jesus Christ, and to love one another as He commanded us. (1 John 3:19–23)

God tells us He expects us to love and believe Him and to love one another. We know when we do those things then we are meeting His expectations. And when we know we are meeting His expectations, then we have boldness in our faith.

Think about This

God has three expectations for us:
Love God
Believe God
Love one another.

We can ask God anything according to His will, and it will be done for us.

Don't forget: There will be times in our lives that Satan will slink around and try to condemn us into believing that God is not happy with us. There will be times our own hearts may try to deceive us into believing a lie. But check out what the Bible has to say:

> God is greater than your heart.
> In your darkest hour.
> During your most desperate plea for forgiveness.
> In your weakest moment.
> God whispers, "I know. And I am greater than your heart"
>   (1 John 3:20).
> Love Him, believe Him, love each other—you meet His
>   every expectation.

Pray

Father God, I am so thankful to know that You aren't disappointed in me and that You don't expect me to do everything right all the time.

I understand clearly from Your Word in Matthew 22:37–39 that You primarily want me to do two things: 1) love and believe You and 2) love others.

Lord, please help me to believe You, even when circumstances make it especially hard. Just like the man in Mark 9:24, I pray, "I do believe; help me overcome my unbelief!"

Knowing that words contain power, please also help me to speak words that agree with Your Word and Your plan so that my heart will be built up to believe You. For Jesus says, "Everything is possible for him who believes" (Mark 9:23).

Secondly, help me to love others—including those who are difficult to love, have hurt me deeply, and/or continue to hurt me. Only You can make this possible. Just like the eleven-year-old girl Kathleen knew, I pray now for you to make the "impossible" possible, by lifting up to You my "impossible to forgive" situations and people:

(*Lift this up to God right now in prayer.*)

Jesus, I understand that as I walk more with You, I will learn to love You more deeply and learn to forgive others more completely. But as I change and grow, I will not allow my heart to condemn just because I "haven't made it yet."

"For the Lord is greater than my heart and He knows (and understands) everything" (1 John 3:20). Amen.

Believe

"Love the Lord your God with all your heart and with all your soul and with all your mind. This is the first and greatest commandment. And the second is like it: 'Love your neighbor as yourself'" (Matt 22:37–39).

"Everything is possible for him who believes. I do believe; help me overcome my unbelief!" (Mark 9:23–24).

"This then is how we know that we belong to the truth, and how we set our hearts at rest in His presence whenever our hearts condemn us. For God is greater than our hearts, and He knows everything. Dear friends, if our hearts do not condemn us, we have confidence before God and receive from Him anything we ask, because we obey His commands and do what pleases Him. And this is His command: to believe in the name of His Son, Jesus Christ, and to love one another as He commanded us" (1 John 3:19–23).

For Journaling and Reflection

1. Have you been under the impression that God will love you more if you do certain things, and love you less if you don't do other things? What are those things? What's the difference between being loved by God unconditionally and trying to earn His love through what you do?

2. It's easy to believe in God's promises with your head, but more difficult with your heart. Think of a situation where you were tempted, deep down, to doubt God's promises for you. What are some words you used at that time that reflect unbelief in those promises? What other words can you replace them with that would affirm His promises for you?

3. When is it hardest for you to believe God's promises?

4. What circumstance, person, or group of people from your past or present do you feel you can't possibly forgive? Can you see how your unforgiveness affects *your* life (with anger, avoidance, bitterness, and inability to trust being critical) and not the other person's?

Eight

Selling Yourself Short
Don't Underestimate Your Worth and Value

There's a story about two teenagers who find a gold and diamond necklace on the sidewalk. Neither had ever seen such a glamorous, expensive necklace.

After celebrating their good luck with joyful high fives, they decided to go to some pawnshops to see how much money they could get for the necklace. They guessed it would sell for hundreds of dollars.

The first pawnshop looked the necklace over and offered them $5,000. Amazed and almost speechless, the teenagers talked it over and decided to go to another pawnshop down the street, just to see if they could do better.

At the second pawnshop, the owner offered the teens $15,000. Getting over their excitement, they decided to try one more store before making the sale.

Finally, they took the necklace to a fancy jewelry store. Right away, the owner offered $30,000.

Already dreaming about how to spend the money, the teens excitedly sold the necklace for $30,000 to the fancy jewelry store.

The next day, on a whim, they decided to go back to the store just to see the necklace displayed. From the sidewalk they could see the necklace and the asking price prominently displayed—$150,000!

Confused and angry, they turned away.

"Guess we coulda gotten more for that necklace," one said.

"Guess so," the other replied.

This story illustrates a very important point: don't underestimate worth and value.

The kids in the story let other people set the worth of the necklace, and then sold it for the highest price. But they got ripped off. The necklace was worth far more than what they received.

In much the same way, many people are waiting to hear from others that they themselves are valuable. Just like the teens in the story, they go from group to group until they've settled on the highest bidder. And even if the group mistreats them, they think that's exactly what they're worth.

This story applies to the cliques at school as much as it does to street gangs. Whatever group you happen to be part of, if you let them determine your value, you'll always be sold short.

Think about This

Only God knows your potential.
Only God knows the hidden talents He's placed within you.
Only God knows your dreams.
Only God knows His plan for you.
Only God knows your heart.
Other people will always sell you short.

In the book of 1 Samuel, God told the prophet Samuel to go pick out the new king of Israel from among the sons of Jesse.

Samuel thought the likeliest candidate was Eliab, the oldest and wisest of all the brothers. Eliab was a warrior, good-looking, strong, and tall.

But the Lord told Samuel, "Do not consider his appearance or his height, for I have rejected him. The Lord does not look at the things man looks at. Man looks at the outward appearance, but the Lord looks at the heart" (1 Sam 16:7).

This is key. Let's read God's opinion again:

"Do not consider his appearance or his height, for I have rejected him. The Lord does not look at the things man looks at. Man looks at the outward appearance, but the Lord looks at the heart."

Is this sinking in? God is looking for someone whose heart is turned toward Him. God will promote that person regardless of his or her outside appearance, age, intelligence, or even abilities.

On with our story: All seven sons of Jesse passed in front of Samuel, but the Lord didn't choose any of them. So Samuel asks Jesse, "Are these all the sons you have?" (1 Sam 16:11). And Jesse replies that there's still one son left—the eighth and youngest one, who's out tending the sheep. That's when Samuel sends for the unlikeliest member of the family. And do you know what happened when the youngest, scrawniest, most inexperienced last of the sons of Jesse was brought in?

Something that astonished everyone. Samuel said, "Rise and anoint him; he is the one" (1 Sam 16:12).

David received honor and glory as the most loved king of Israel, but not because he had the best education, or because he was the best-looking, or because he was the best connected.

It was because day after day and year after year, while tending the sheep out in the fields, David listened to God and poured out his heart to Him. David's heart was turned toward God.

God chose David because God looked at David's heart and liked what He saw: "a man after his own heart." And God appointed David as leader of His people (1 Sam13:14).

God noticed David even when no one else did.

Probably no one ever told David he was a smart kid or he was doing a good job. And David had never won an award before he was given the highest honor in the land as king of all of Israel. But David didn't do things to win the approval of people. David got his value and worth from His Heavenly Father. David's heart was turned toward God.

Think about This

Just like David, God gives us our value, and He never sells us short. He gives us a value far beyond what we even deserve. We can only get our true value from listening to God. He will never sell us short.

Consider this parable that Jesus told: "Again, the kingdom of heaven is like a merchant looking for fine pearls. When he found one of great value, he went away and sold everything he had and bought it" (Matt 13:45–46).

Who was that merchant looking for fine pearls? Although the parable can be interpreted in many ways, one meaning is that God is the merchant looking for fine pearls.

So who are the pearls? We are the pearls. We have great value to God. God created people to have a super-close relationship with Him. But Adam and Eve sold out. As in the parable of the pearl, God went away and sold everything and bought us.

Here's what he did: God gave His only Son to purchase our redemption, so we could have a close relationship with God on this earth and live forever with Him in Heaven. Now that's what the Kingdom of Heaven is like.

Look at it this way:

> Again, the Kingdom of Heaven is like a merchant [God] looking for fine pearls [us]. When he found one of great value, He went away and sold everything He had [Jesus died] and bought it [Jesus rose from the dead and paid the price for our redemption]. (Matt 13:45–46)

Now let's put this parable together with 1 Corinthians 6:20 and see what God might say to our hearts.

1 Corinthians 6:20 says, "You were bought at a price."

Bought by whom? The Great Merchant, God.

At what price? A great expense—His Own Son's death.

Look at the word "price." It's translated from the Greek word *time* (pronounced tee-may') meaning "honor, price, sum, precious." The Greek word for price refers to a valuing by which the price is fixed, to the price itself, to the price paid or received for a person or thing bought or sold, or even to the honor given to a person.

In other words, God paid the highest price for you. He honors you. And He calls you valuable and worth it.

Let's tie this all in with 1 Corinthians 7:23: "You were bought at a price; do not become slaves of men."

What does God mean by "slaves of men"?

Not surprisingly, the Greek word for "men" is *anthropos* (pronounced anth'-ro-pos). Look familiar? *Anthropos* means a human being, whether male or female.

The Greek word for men refers to the two-fold nature of man: body and soul—which includes our physical and emotional needs.

Anthropos (men) also means "merchantmen"—referring to a market-place of buying and selling.

Let's reread 1 Corinthians 7:23 with a little more insight: "You were bought at a price; do not become slaves of men."

You were purchased with great honor—a precious price, the writer of the letter to the Corinthians seems to be saying. Don't become a slave to any person, opinion, or marketplace. Don't rely on your own emotions or feelings to give you your value or worth. Don't let TV, magazines, or any crowd you hang around with give you your value or dictate your worth.

As a human race, we have a disastrous habit of selling ourselves to the highest bidder. Perhaps one crowd rejected us, so we join another. Perhaps we aren't valued anywhere, so we decide to depend only on ourselves.

Every time you do any of that, you sell yourself short.

Only God knows your great value. And He proved His point by giving His Son to die for you.

Be like David. Be content in your own "shepherd's field." God isn't looking for the best looking or the smartest or even the wisest because "the LORD does not look at the things man looks at. Man looks at the outward appearance, but the LORD looks at the heart" (1 Sam 16:7).

God is looking for men and women after His own heart. God gives you great value.

Pray

Dear Jesus, please teach me my worth in You. Please help me not to look to another person, the media, my own feelings (my past or even what I am capable of today) in order to get my value.

God, I really need help in this area, and I'm depending on You to help me to do this.

Also God, in many ways I feel as though I am in a shepherd's field doing the same things every day, but wanting change. Sometimes I am really lonely. I am trusting You to teach me and give me joy in those times. I trust that in Your timing, I will be all You have created me to be. Amen.

Believe

"The Lord does not look at the things man looks at. Man looks at the outward appearance, but the Lord looks at the heart" (1 Sam 16:7).

"Again, the Kingdom of Heaven is like a merchant looking for fine pearls. When he found one of great value, he went away and sold everything he had and bought it" (Matt 13:45–46).

"You were bought at a price; do not become slaves of men" (1 Cor 7:23).

For Journaling and Reflection

1. Think about the ways you've looked to someone or something else (from clothing to lifestyle, music to social cliques, diets to boyfriends) to validate or define who you are. Which of these are good ways to help discover your true identity? Which are not?

2. How important is it for you to earn someone else's approval? Have you ever compromised who you really are or sold yourself short, just to please someone else who may not have your best interests at heart?

3. Is there someone whose value you're underestimating in your life? What might be keeping you from appreciating their worthiness and what can you do to show them their value in your life?

Nine

Distant from God

Finding Your Way Back

Why do we sometimes feel close to God and other times far away from Him?

Feeling distanced from God isn't a good feeling, and there's no easy answer for why it happens. Sometimes we feel distanced from God when we're not doing or saying the right things. Maybe we aren't being bad—just a little off-center.

Sometimes our schedules get so hectic that we only give a little time to God. And we seem to run from one task to the next and never feel like we're accomplishing anything.

During frenzied times, we feel as though we're putting out fires, chasing our tails, and even searching for ways to console ourselves. We might find ourselves saying things like: "Maybe I need a vacation. Maybe I need someone to listen to me. Maybe I need to get more organized. Maybe I need a hot shower. Maybe I need . . ."

At times like this, we try to get peace any way we can, because we sense a need we cannot fill when we feel distanced from God.

And when we feel distanced from God, we feel we're forever trying! Trying to quit, trying to start, trying to be, trying not to be, trying to learn, trying to forget—always trying.

As a matter of fact, we're trying so hard that we get tired and begin to notice that people around us, many of whom aren't even trying to please God, seem much more carefree and happy that we are. "What's the deal?" we begin to wonder. We may not know other people's private thoughts and struggles, and we have no idea what God is doing in their lives, but that doesn't stop us from wondering why we're struggling and unhappy while others seem to be happy and carefree.

Sometimes, friends and family—and even strangers—come to us with problems and ask us for prayers and advice. It's a joy to be able to help others like this, but when we feel distanced from God this joy becomes a burden, and our minds become loaded with all the difficult situations we should be carrying to Our Heavenly Father.

Has anyone ever unloaded a big problem on you when you felt distanced from God? What do you do? Do you crack open your Bible and see if it lands on a Scripture passage that seems to apply? Do you start a prayer, "Dear God, I know we haven't talked in a while, but . . ." Or do you just try to be a good listener and then later feel overwhelmed with more things to pray for?

If we keep walking near to God, then we simply hand the problem to Him. But if we've wandered away from Him, and sense the distance between us, then we must first go on a God-search before we can hand over any situations.

Feeling distanced from God makes us feel empty, off-center, overloaded, and frustrated. And, it's sad to say, there have been times when I've blamed God for feeling distanced from Him. I've even tried to ignore Him for a while.

But one of the most miraculous things about being a Christian is the fact that once you've chosen Jesus and asked Him to be your Lord and to be your Savior, Jesus promises to never leave you. No matter how you act toward the Lord, He'll always be there, waiting for you.

Deuteronomy 31:6 says, "Be strong and courageous. Do not be afraid or terrified because of them, for the LORD your God goes with you; He will never leave you nor forsake you."

Every day we hear about marriages that have split, business partners parting on a sour note, best friends going separate ways, and even children divorcing their parents. Our world is a world of conditional love. We're immersed in it. We live it.

People seem to say: "I'll love you as long as you don't disappoint me. I'll love you if you agree with me. I'll love you if you never betray me. I'll love you if you accept me. I'll love you if you approve of me. I'll love you if you love me back." In other words, "I'll love you as long as you meet all of my standards and conditions for love."

But God is different. He completely and wholly loves you and me even when we're not acting right. He loves us the same whether we're spending an hour with Him every day or an hour with Him over the course of a year.

God loved you when you didn't love Him. And He loved you while you were doing your most shameful, embarrassing, or stupid things. God loves you!

When my daughter started school, I was introduced to time-outs. When kids misbehave, they're asked to sit away from their classmates. Most of us who have experienced "time-outs" as children think we're punished with time-outs from God when we don't live our lives as we ought to. We imagine that if our performance isn't up to par, God must give a little nod to an angel, who subtly removes us from group play and lifts us to the corner of the room, where we stare at a wall and contemplate our mistakes. When enough time has passed, the angel allows us to quietly reenter the activity and watches to see that we modify our behavior to meet all of God's standards.

Time-outs may work in preschool, but that's not how God operates. No matter what we do—or what we don't do—God never sits us in a corner and removes us from His loving presence. If we feel distant from God, it's not because God is a little irked at our antics and put us in a corner alone. The distance we feel is however far we have walked away from God. So why doesn't He chase us down and pull us back to Him?

Even as I ask the question, a two-part answer settles over me.

Answer #1: He does . . .

Answer #2: He doesn't . . .

God chases us every day with the blessings around us. The little robin singing outside your window as you got dressed wasn't a little mistake of nature. God sent that little bird to you just as He sent that little warm breeze to tickle your neck the evening before. And the full moon? He sent that so your eyes would gaze heavenward as you stopped to breathe in His goodness and contemplate the beauty of His stars.

It was God who prompted the friend who sent you a kind and encouraging email just when you needed it. And God who directed you to the new kid in your school who needed a word of welcome. Finally, it was God who opened up your schedule when you unconsciously offered up a silent prayer saying you didn't even have an hour to be with Him. And God waited patiently during that hour for a chance to be with you as you felt sorry for yourself, bored, and even a little angry because you didn't have anyone to do fun things with.

I know ignoring God must hurt Him. And yet, all during all my wanderings in life, He's always been there to comfort me, sent angels to wipe my tears and collect them in His bottle, when maybe I should have been noticing His. (Psalm 56:8 [KJV]: "Thou tellest my wanderings: put Thou my tears into Thy bottle: are they not in Thy book?")

Maybe we've all had a tiny taste of how God might feel when we reject His love. Have you ever reached out in love to a person again and again but been rejected again and again? Do you remember how that feels? That's probably how it feels for God when we reject Him. Love rejected hurts to the core of your being. If it happens too much, it gets harder and harder to love.

But not for God! For God, love repetitively rejected is given again and again.

This is God's very nature—to love. No matter how many times we've rejected God's love, when we tell Him we're sorry, He says, "Forgiven!"

So why does He let us walk away from Him in the first place? Does God chase us when we wander from Him? I've explained that He does. Let me also explain that He doesn't.

Remember the story of the prodigal son? You know, some people might not relate to that story because they haven't wandered deep into sin like the young man in the story. But I think the story isn't so much about the degree of sin that the young man committed, but about how his father responded. The father gives the young man his inheritance just because he asked for it—just as we are only given our inheritance in Christ—our salvation—when we ask for it. But no sooner did the young man receive his inheritance than he went off and spent it all in wild living. The young man wandered to the "bad side of town," walking away from a loving father who didn't run after him. There's nothing in the story about a search team formed to drag the son back home and put him in time-out. There's nothing in the story about the father sending messages to tell the son how disappointed he was. There's nothing in the story about the father disinheriting his wayward child.

Think about This

Jesus told this story—we call it a parable—about a wandering son to show us how our Father God treats us, His sons and daughters, when we wander.

As Christians, we need to understand this because if we are to become God's messengers to one of His wandering children, we'd better be sure we're giving them the right message.

When we meet people who are wandering from God's love, it's our job to remind them that God loves them no matter what, even though we may need to also offer a word of warning. But it's never our job to put another child of God in a time-out. God doesn't shun us for our transgressions, so we shouldn't shun others.

The father simply waited for the son to come to his senses and to realize that he needed his father. Isn't that just what God does with us? He sometimes has to let us hit rock bottom, recognize our frustrations, come to our senses, and realize our emptiness. Here's what the Bible says about the wandering son: "When he came to his senses, he said, 'How many of my father's hired men have food to spare, and here I am starving to death! I will set out and go back to my father and say to him: Father, I have sinned against heaven and against you'" (Luke 15:17–18).

That son really knew his dad. He knew the big deal wasn't about the money he had lost or the lifestyle he had led. He knew that he had created a chasm in their relationship when he wandered away from his father and wasted his inheritance. Yet he knew he could come home.

Do you know your Heavenly Father? Do you know He is patiently waiting for you to come to your senses? He eagerly awaits. And like the wandering son in the story, God, the Father, wants your simple acknowledgment it isn't that you let the group down, or let yourself down, or let your family down. It's that you walked away from your Heavenly Dad. The prodigal son did come to senses and return to his father: "So he [the prodigal son] got up and went to his father. But while he was still a long way off, his father saw him and was filled with compassion for him; he ran to his son, threw his arms around him and kissed him" (Luke 15:20).

Look at those words again. When did the father become filled with compassion and run and kiss his son? While he was still a *long way* off— and *before* the son had done anything to earn his forgiveness. He hadn't won back his father's trust. He hadn't earned back his father's love.

He had always had it. He was the son.

In the same way, if we take one step in God's direction, He runs to hug and kiss us even while we're still a long way off. He waits for us. In all circumstances, or every step we take toward God, God will take many giant steps toward us.

Every day, we have a choice: to wander away from God, or to walk with Him. And the choice we make depends on what or whom we seek.

In the Greek language that this Gospel story was written in, the word "seek" is expressed by the word *zeteo* (dzay-teh'-o), which means "to seek, to go about, and to desire." It implies to seek in order to find, to seek a thing, to seek (in order to find out by thinking, meditating, reasoning), to enquire into, to seek after, seek for, aim at, strive after, to require, to demand, and to crave. Think of this Greek definition of seek when you read this passage: "But seek first His Kingdom and His righteousness, and all these things will be given to you as well" (Matt 6:33). In other words, if I ask the Holy Spirit within me to help me to first seek God (crave, meditate, desire, aim at, and go after God first), then every other thing I need will be added to me. Seek Him first, and I'll be walking close beside Him on the road of blessing. Seek other things first, and I'll be wandering down the path, looking for the blessings, working for the promises, and wondering: Why do I feel so distant from God?

Pray

Father, I am sometimes like the prodigal son who was given so much and still wandered off and squandered it on worthless things. Father, I too have sinned against Heaven and against You. I want to take that step now in seeking You first. Thank You that You are filled with compassion for me and run toward me even when I've wandered a long way off.

Jesus, teach me to crave, desire, go after, aim for, and seek first You and Your Kingdom. I know when I seek You first, good things will be added unto me, even though I don't even deserve them.

Lord, I hate wandering. Guide me, Holy Spirit, in Your Truths and Your ways. Teach me how to spend joyous times walking beside You all the days of my life. Amen.

Believe

"So he got up and went to his father. But while he was still a long way off, his father saw him and was filled with compassion for him; he ran to his son, threw his arms around him and kissed him" (Luke 15:20).

"But seek first His Kingdom and His righteousness, and all these things will be given to you as well" (Matt 6:33).

For Journaling and Reflection

1. If you've ever felt distanced from God, did you recognize that's what it was? How did you feel? What did you do to bring yourself closer to Him?

2. In what ways do you feel like you've been loved conditionally by others? What conditions have you set up for those you love?

3. What sweet, personal blessings has God chased you with this week?

4. Do you feel like the prodigal son (or daughter) right now? Do you know someone who might have wandered from God's love? Do you believe that either of you can come home any time, your Heavenly Father doesn't love you any less, and He will run out to meet you? If not, why not? What's the first step you can take in your life that will put you back on the road home?

Ten

God's Timing; God's Ways
Trusting God during the Wait

A friend sent me this email:

> A young man once asked God how long a million years was to Him.
>
> God replied, "A million years to Me is just like a single second to you."
>
> The young man asked God what a million dollars was to Him.
>
> God replied, "A million dollars to Me is just like a single penny to you."
>
> Then the young man got his courage up and asked, "God, could I have one of Your pennies?"
>
> God smiled and replied, "Certainly, just a second."

This e-mail joke illustrates a very important point: God's timing is not our timing!

God's timing isn't like human timing at all. For example, in the early days of the church, after Jesus' resurrection and ascension into heaven, many Christians believed that Christ would quickly return to earth. But it's been over two thousand years, and He still hasn't come back.

Two thousand years is approximately twenty-two to thirty generations. That's a long time to wait. Yet the Bible says that Christ is returning soon. That means that soon to us isn't soon to God.

On the other hand, late to us isn't late to God either. For example, Hebrews 10:37 says that Jesus will return and "not tarry." (The word "tarry" means to wait, stay, loiter, dally, linger, or put off.)

In our human understanding, waiting for over two thousand years is definitely putting something off.

So if it's been two thousand years, why hasn't Christ come back to earth?

That's simple: Because our timing is not God's timing!

Seconds to God may be years to us, while a lifetime to us may be a mere breath of time to God. So sometimes God's timing can seem too short, but usually God's timing seems to take too long.

Have you been waiting for God to do something for a long, long time? Does it seem like it will never happen? Maybe you're waiting to meet one true friend who really understands you. Maybe you're waiting to find the right person to date. Maybe you are waiting for God to help you make a very important decision. Maybe you're waiting to see what God wants you to do with your life. Maybe you're waiting to be healed.

Maybe you've grown tired of waiting and negative thoughts have come to your mind such as: "Maybe I'll never get what I have been waiting for."

Maybe you are close to giving up . . .

God has something to tell you:

> Do not throw away your confidence; it will be richly rewarded. You need to persevere so that when you have done the will of God, you will receive what He has promised. For in just a very little while, "He who is coming will come and will not delay. But My righteous one will live by faith. And if he shrinks back, I will not be pleased with him." (Heb 10:35–38)

God is telling us (and we are His children that He sent His Son to die for) to keep trusting Him even while we wait.

God's timing is very different than our timing. His ways are different than our ways. As a matter of fact, the Bible says God's timing and His ways are not only different than ours, they are also higher than ours.

> "For My thoughts are not your thoughts, neither are your ways My ways, saith the LORD. For as the heavens are higher than the earth, so are My ways higher than your ways, and My thoughts than your thoughts." (Isa 55:8–9, KJV)

"Higher" in Hebrew is the word *gabahh* (gaw-bah'), meaning "more exalted and more excellent."

So if we replaced the word "higher" in the Scripture with "more exalted" and "more excellent," then the passage in Isaiah 55:8–9 would read: "For My thoughts are not your thoughts, neither are your ways My ways, saith the LORD. For as the heavens are [more exalted and more excellent] than the earth, so are My ways [more exalted and more excellent] than your ways, and My thoughts than your thoughts."

What is God telling us? That we'll always understand His ways? No.

God is telling us His ways are more exalted and more excellent than our ways. And He is telling us His timing is different than our timing (Isa 55:8–9), but if we hold on and trust Him then our confidence "will be richly rewarded . . . and [we] will receive what He has promised" (Heb 10:35–38).

Several years ago I wrote this little true story.

———

"The Bus Stop"

Yesterday, Mattie (my five-year-old) went out to the bus stop near our house at the regular time, 7:40 a.m. and waited for the bus. I was in a hurry, I had to meet the contractor at 8:15, needed to shower, return a lot of phone calls, and then go to Bible study.

We waited for the bus, and we waited for the bus. No bus. I began to wonder, "Did the bus come really early and I missed it?" That couldn't be. The bus always came about 7:50, but it was past 8:00, and we had waited (with mud all around for Mattie to get into) for over thirty minutes.

"This is ridiculous!" I was getting nervous, so I thought I would just take her to school, and then I remembered I didn't have keys to my husband's car. He had taken my Tahoe to pick up fertilizer for the yard. That made me really frustrated. I became irked at him for taking my car and not leaving me the keys.

We waited a little longer.

I paced; Mattie swung.

I mumbled; Mattie hummed.

I decided I had to know if we had missed the bus. So I told Mattie to stay where she was, and I jogged up three or four blocks to see if any other people were waiting. They were all gone. I began to jog back in a huff. I thought, "I got up at 5:00 a.m. so my busy, busy day would run smoothly. I didn't plan for this. How could the bus have come early and left Mattie? What is going on? Where is Lacey when I need him? Why is Mattie in the mud? What if I don't have time to talk to the contractor?"

While mulling this over, two blocks from home I see the trusty yellow school bus pull up to our curb, and Mattie waves and steps on. The people at the next stop were gone because they thought they had been left and drove to school.

Instantly the Holy Spirit said to me, "I will never leave you or forsake you. You will not miss the bus unless you walk away from the bus stop. Sometimes I will appear early and sometimes I will appear late, but I will always be on My time. You can wait patiently and in peace, or you can wait anxiously and worry. But know that I will never ever leave you at the bus stop. I will always come for you to take you where you need to be."

God was speaking to me so clearly about waiting to receive 100 percent healing from chronic back pain from the metal rod in my spine. The devil had been saying, "It has been twenty years of excruciating pain. What makes you think God is going to show up now?" And I had begun to lose hope and faith.

But God has done so many miracles in my life: healed of leukemia, fulfilling my desire to be Christian speaker, a wonderful family, incredible friends. He has always come through for me.

Wait at the bus stop. Swing. Hum. Enjoy the green grass and the blue sky. Give God your schedule. Give God your dreams. Give God your pain.

He is coming. And He is always on His time.

You see, almost exactly twenty years ago, doctors had to put a full-length stainless steel rod and two hooks in my spine because of scoliosis. Not one day went by from age thirteen to age thirty-four that I did not experience moderate to severe pain.

For twenty years, including the time I wrote "The Bus Stop," my back hurt severely day and night. I went to many doctors, prayed, and fasted, and was anointed with oil in order to be healed.

For twenty years.

Until a special small prayer group I am in began to fervently pray for answers. Several months later, we were able to remove the upper hook from my spine and do a series of epidural steroid injections to block nerve pain. I am so much better—it was worth the wait! And one year before publishing this book, I had another back surgery that fused the remaining three discs of my back, relieving me from severe nerve pain.

God's timing is not our timing. His ways are not our ways. But I am so thankful to Him.

My back is completely fused now (I can only bend my neck), and I am still uncomfortable sitting. But I am trusting God to take care of all that too—and any other problem that comes my way.

People have speculated for generations why certain things happen. I feel secure in saying, "I don't know."

I feel secure in believing Isaiah 55:8–9—that God's ways are more excellent than mine—and I could give countless examples in my life and the lives of other believers where God looked like He wasn't working, but He was. And the end result was unspeakable joy.

As I write these words, my daughter Mattie is twelve years old and my son Storm is five. And I am living my dream—to have a wonderful husband and children and to write and speak about our loving Heavenly Father.

Pray

Dear Heavenly Father, I choose to trust You today. I choose to trust You with what I cannot see. I choose to trust You when all looks lost. I choose to trust You when I am in pain. I choose to trust You when my heart is broken.

Jesus, I desperately need Your strength, courage, and love. I am an overcomer because of You. I overcome evil with good. ("Do not be overcome by evil, but overcome evil with good" [Rom 12:21].) And I trust You to help me overcome all the negative situations in my life.

Holy Spirit, please minister to me Your peace so I can wait on the perfect timing of God and trust in His ways, knowing they are above my own. Amen.

Believe

"So do not throw away your confidence; it will be richly rewarded. You need to persevere so that when you have done the will of God, you will receive what He has promised. For in just a very little while, 'He who is coming will come and will not delay. But My righteous one will live by faith. And if he shrinks back, I will not be pleased with him'" (Heb 10:35–38).

"For My thoughts are not your thoughts, neither are your ways My ways, saith the Lord. For as the heavens are higher than the earth, so are My ways higher than your ways, and My thoughts than your thoughts" (Isa 55:8–9, KJV).

"Do not be overcome by evil, but overcome evil with good" (Rom 12:21).

For Journaling and Reflection

1. Think back on your life to when God's timing was definitely *not* your timing. Are you glad now that God didn't seem to answer your prayer the way you would have liked at the time? Was there something you really wanted then, but are so grateful you *didn't* get in hindsight?

2. Read again what God says in Romans 10:35–38. God's will is that you live your life by faith, staying confident that His timing is perfect. What character trait have you noticed God nurturing and developing in you as you wait for His perfect will to unfold (flexibility, patience, faith, hope, maturity, trust, or even a deeper relationship with Him)?

Eleven

Everyone Judging Anyone

Freedom from Condemnation

Public speaking can be a funny thing. It's a lot like life: You're never sure what to expect—and the audience isn't either.

Many times groups invite me to speak without having seen me. Some assume I look this way or act that way, and when I don't fit their expectations, some have actually said, "Gee, we thought you were (older, taller, wider, wilder, calmer, more talkative, less talkative . . .). You get the picture.

But interestingly, most people go on to say, "But we're so glad you are who you are, because your message of God's love really spoke to our hearts."

Public speaking is just like life. We all have certain preconceived notions or images about the people around us. We have first impressions, second impressions, and even third impressions, but that's all they are—impressions.

And even as we get beyond impressions and get to know people on the inside, we still don't ever really know everything about them—even if they're family members or close friends.

Hold that thought. Let's turn to a very dangerous activity. Not sky diving or race car driving: What I'm thinking of can actually be much more dangerous that that. And yet most of us do it every day. It's called: figuring someone out.

I've heard people say—I've even heard myself say, "I really can't figure out So-and-So. So-and-So seems to be blah blah blah blah. What do you think So-and-So is thinking? Why do you think So-and-So did that?"

This practice of figuring someone out is dangerous territory for several reasons.

Think about This

Any time we try to analyze or even guess the motives of another, then we are judging them—and judging others always brings a big "Don't Go There!" from God. "Be merciful, just as your Father is merciful. Do not judge, and you will not be judged. Do not condemn, and you will not be condemned. Forgive, and you will be forgiven" (Luke 6:36–37).

Life is complicated enough when we try to figure out ourselves. It would be exhausting to try to figure out anyone else. Half the time we don't even know why we do the things we do—how could we ever know why someone else does something?

When it comes to another person, we never have the full picture. There's always missing information. No one but God can know the whole story, grasp the big picture, or understand heart motives.

No one except God. Check out this Scripture passage:

> "And you, my son Solomon, acknowledge the God of your father, and serve Him with wholehearted devotion and with a willing mind, for the LORD searches every heart and understands every motive behind the thoughts." (1 Chron 28:9)

Only God can understand motives behind our thoughts. Only God understands our past experiences, our secret fears, our private dreams, and our intimate prayers.

Recently, I had a great discussion with a group of women about how freeing it is to realize that everyone's opinion doesn't matter. Isn't it strange that through our whole lives there has been this ominous being called *everyone*—although no one can tell *anyone* who *everyone* is.

"I can't wear that. Everyone will think I'm stupid."

"God, I'm not sure I can do what You are asking me to do. What will everyone think?"

Does any of this sound familiar?

I wish we had a T-shirt that said, "Who's Everyone?"

Two things I've learned: Everyone isn't the one that matters. We can't judge anyone.

One time I drove several hours in heavy fog and light drizzle to speak in a nearby city. I finally arrived at a bank building that was to be the setting for the business women's meeting. I was greeted by a distinguished group of women who formed the welcoming committee that checked off names as people entered.

I walked up to the first lady in the line and told her my name. She was looking at the lower half of my body and didn't appear to be paying attention, so I repeated myself. "Hello," I said. "My name is Kathleen Whitten."

This time, her eyes traveled from my heels to my skirt (I began to worry that she thought it was too short) and then up to my hair.

Somewhat shocked, I repeated my name a third time and added, "I'm the speaker for your meeting."

"Oh!" another lady at the next table exclaimed. "Oh, well, of course we're so glad you're here," she said as she got up, almost knocking over the welcome table.

"You'll want to freshen up I'm sure," she continued. "Uh, don't you think that it would be a good idea for our speaker to freshen up before we begin?" She addressed the other hostesses.

Everyone murmured yes, and I heard a chorus of, "Please, do feel free to freshen up." The first lady still hadn't even acknowledged my presence.

On the way to the bathroom, I felt relatively sure something was glaringly wrong with my appearance. Maybe I was much younger than they expected. Maybe my skirt *was* too short. Maybe I had something awful between my teeth. I mulled this over in the ladies room while washing my hands. The door opened, and the original unwelcoming hostess walked up to the sink and began to wash her hands.

Now I was challenged. I could ignore her as she had rudely ignored me, or I could make another attempt at being friendly. I decided to chat about the safest possible subject—the weather. "It was really foggy on the drive here," I heard myself say, "but that's okay, 'cause I kinda like driving in the fog. I like driving in the rain too, but I'm glad we aren't in a downpour right now."

Not so subtly, and without even glancing my way, she reached for a paper towel, dried her hands, and exited the bathroom.

You know, a lot of things go through your mind when you're treated like dirt. I thought about packing up and going home, but my stomach was growling and they were serving lunch, but more importantly I believed that welcome or not, God had sent me with a message—ironically, a message about His love.

So after running several ridiculous scenarios in my mind: leaving, going up to the podium and talking about rudeness, pinning my skirt up even shorter, or condensing my one-hour message to a quick five minutes, I finally decided to pray.

"God, I know You sent me to these women to bring a message from You. But God, they don't even *like* me. Please make Your love shine through me in a way they will understand. Amen."

No sooner had I prayed than I heard a voice inside me say, "If you speak directly to her, she will hear you."

"Okay," I said out loud, not even caring if anyone was in the bathroom stalls and heard. "I'll do what you say, God."

Even as I left the ladies room, my mind was churning. "You don't even know where she is sitting in that crowd, how can you 'talk directly' to her?" But as I headed toward the front table, I passed her. She was the table hostess of one of the front and center tables facing mine.

After the usual introductions, I began my talk. But for the first time in my speaking career, I spoke almost as if I were addressing only one person. The etiquette of public speaking requires that you scan the room with your gaze as you talk. Instead, I faced the unwelcoming hostess for every important comment. I directed my attention to her and did my best to talk directly to her without being too obvious.

And something began to happen. As I talked, she slowly melted and came alive. She laughed at my jokes! And she teared up when I described something touching. She clasped her hands in front of her face during suspenseful descriptions and frowned in contemplation when I talked about the depth of God's love for us. She even smiled—no, beamed—when I described Christ's love and forgiveness for us all. And I knew God was right: When I spoke directly to her, she really got it!

After the luncheon, several women approached, and she was among them.

While another lady was talking to me, I saw her friend lean toward the now-beaming "unwelcoming hostess," tap her on the shoulder, and say very clearly and slowly, "Could you understand the speaker?" And very slowly, very methodically, but with great joy, she answered her friend, "I huh-rd ev-er-y wuhrd."

The woman was hearing impaired.

I cried on the way home after the meeting.

I cried because God is so wise and I am not. God told me that if I spoke right to her, then she would hear me because she needed to read my lips.

I cried because I had judged someone and I was so wrong.

I cried because I had made a new friend.

And I cried because God showed me how to speak so that my new friend would hear.

I learned in a very real way that day we don't always see the full picture or hear the whole story.

I learned not only do we not always speak the same language, but some of us hear the same language in a different way.

All of us truly need God to direct us in communicating, understanding, and loving one another. This is part of our human need. This is life.

Pray

Dear Jesus, please forgive me for the times I have judged another. I recognize that only You can know the intentions of someone's heart, and it is wrong for me to judge anyone. I ask You now to please bless this person(s) I have judged, misunderstood, or harbored bitterness against.

Forgive me also, Lord, for putting too much emphasis on what everyone else thinks or does. Truly Your opinion matters the most. Help me, please, to live my life in a way that allows You to shine through. Help me communicate Your love in a language people will understand. Help me, please, to keep from feeling offended or touchy. God, please mold me into someone you can use. Amen.

Believe

"Be ye therefore merciful, as your Father also is merciful. Judge not, and ye shall not be judged: condemn not, and ye shall not be condemned: forgive, and ye shall be forgiven" (Luke 6:36–37, KJV).

"And you, my son Solomon, acknowledge the God of your father, and serve Him with wholehearted devotion and with a willing mind, for the LORD searches every heart and understands every motive behind the thoughts" (1 Chron 28:9).

For Journaling and Reflection

1. What's the last thing you did (or didn't do) or say because you were concerned about what "everyone" would think?
2. Have you ever misjudged someone or something and been so wrong about it, after thinking you were so right? Has someone ever been that wrong about you? Think about how forgiveness can work a miracle in both scenarios.
3. What are some ways you can give people the benefit of the doubt the next time they misjudge you—for instance, you might imagine that they're having a really bad day or that they misunderstood what you said.

Twelve

Book of Remembrance

Acknowledging God's Goodness

Did you know God is thrilled when you talk about Him? And did you know God keeps a Book of Remembrance to record every time you get together with others to talk about Him?

This includes the time you e-mailed your best friend about the good changes God is making in your life. And the time you sat around the table in the school cafeteria and listened to your classmates' stories about how God's forgiveness turned bad situations into good ones. What about the time you shared some Scripture verses with kids who were worried and told them that they could always trust God?

Did you know God is writing all this good talk down?

Well, He is. Check out this Bible verse:

> "Then they that feared the LORD spake often one to another: and the LORD hearkened, and heard it, and a book of remembrance was written before Him for them that feared the LORD, and that thought upon His name." (Mal 3:16, KJV)

God has a book of remembrance because when you talk good about Him, it brings joy to His heart.

It brings encouragement to God, Jesus, the Holy Spirit, the angels, and even our great cloud of witnesses—believers who have gone to Heaven before us—to read and reread that Book of Remembrance.

So here is my suggestion: Do something God does. Keep a Book of Remembrance.

Think about This

Designate a special notebook or folder or even a blank journal as your Book of Remembrance. But record only those things you are thankful for.

This will be your Book of Remembrance of how God has blessed you, answered your prayers, delivered you, rescued you, saved you, given you favor, helped you, and done miraculous things for you.

Many people keep journals. This is not a journal.

A Book of Remembrance isn't about what you're praying for or what you've done. A book of Remembrance is about what you're thankful for and what God has done.

Recently I've started taking my little book with me to dinner when I go out with my husband. We used to spend half of our date time talking about all the little problems in our lives that we needed to ask God to help us solve. Now we spend time talking instead about things we are thankful God has done over the past few weeks. It's interesting: I usually learn a lot of things God has done for my husband that I would never have known otherwise.

Take your remembrance book with you to dinner with your family. Ask them to share times when God has answered their prayers recently. Throw your Book of Remembrance into your purse or backpack so that during the day you can jot down your messy thanks. If you try to wait for a quiet moment when you can neatly organize your thoughts, then your book will remain blank.

And when you're discouraged, reread your little Book of Remembrance. It will remind you that if God has already helped you, then He'll help you again and again. If you feel sad, read your Book of Remembrance and remember things can turn around and really get better. Read your book when circumstances don't look very good and remember this: "Jesus is the same yesterday and today and forever" (Heb 13:8).

Here are a few passages from my own book of remembrance:

> From junior school: "God, even though I was kind of nervous about it at first, thank You for getting me moved to a new school where people seem to be interested in me for who I really am."
>
> From high school: "God, I am so thankful that You have given me friends of other faiths and that they have seen through my triumphs and mistakes that You are real to me."
>
> From college: "Well, God, it looks like You are answering my prayer (that I didn't want to have a string of 'going nowhere relationships') because Lacey is talking about engagement."
>
> From a recent entry: "Lord, You have done so much in my life. How could I ever doubt? You brought me a wonderful husband, Lacey, allowed me to give birth (even with a full-length metal rod) to a beautiful, artistic daughter, Mattie. You healed me of leukemia and fulfilled a lifelong dream to adopt a son, Storm, from an orphanage in a destitute country. And today? I love my family, speaking about You and now writing a book for girls. Who would have *ever* thought You could do anything through the mousy little girl with the crooked spine who everyone used to make fun of. I want everyone to know You like I do!"

Remember God's great love for you shown in the blessings of everyday life—the friend who text messages you to cheer you up one evening when you're feeling low, or the teacher who wrote an encouraging comment on your homework paper—and perhaps you'll treasure your little Book of Remembrance about God, just as Heaven treasures God's Book of Remembrance about you.

Pray

God, please make in me a thankful heart
for all that You have done.
For giving me breath and life and for giving me Your Son.
All my days should be filled with praise
but often I fill them with fear.
Please help me Lord, to see beyond my needs
and thank You for Your blessings
already here.
Amen.

Believe

"Then they that feared [loved and revered] the LORD spake often one to another: and the LORD hearkened, and heard it, and a book of remembrance was written before Him for them that feared the LORD, and that thought upon His name" (Mal 3:16, KJV).

"Create in me a clean heart, O God; and renew a right spirit within me. Cast me not away from Thy presence; and take not Thy holy spirit from me. Restore unto me the joy of Thy salvation; and uphold me with Thy free spirit" (Ps 51:10–12, KJV).

"For the joy of the LORD is your strength" (Neh 8:10, KJV).

"And now, behold, I go bound in the spirit unto Jerusalem, not knowing the things that shall befall me there: Save the Holy Ghost witnessing in every city, saying that bonds and afflictions abide me. But none of these things move me, neither count I my life dear unto myself, so that I might finish my course with joy, and the ministry, which I have received of the Lord Jesus, to testify the gospel of the grace of God" (Acts 20:22–24, KJV).

For Journaling and Reflection

1. If you were to start your Book of Remembrance at this moment, what three things would top your list? Jot them down in your journal or in the margins of this book right now, and say a quick prayer of thanks for the blessings these things represent in your life.

2. When you're hanging out with friends or family, what topics do your conversations center around? Name a few ways you could steer the conversation toward things you're thankful for rather than problems you're working through.

3. How can you help encourage someone who is focusing on their problems to see how God has—and always will—come through for them?

4. The next time you're in need of hope or cheering up, in what ways can you help remind yourself of God's faithfulness to you in the past?

Thirteen

Bank on It

Growing Your Faith

Once there was a very young boy who had a few coins. He was so excited about his new treasure that he didn't want to lose even one of them, so he decided to make a little bank to put them in.

Day after day he tried different ways to build a little bank around his coins. First, he tried molding clay around the coins, but that only made a mess. Next, he tried weaving reeds around his coins, but the reeds ended up in knots, and his coins ended up on the floor.

Finally, he put the coins on a small piece of plywood and built a miniature wooden bank around them. It was wonderful to have a little bank, and his coins fit perfectly.

But it wasn't long before his grandparents gave him more coins, and the boy's bank became too small. Being an industrious little boy, he opened his miniature bank, took out the coins, placed them on a bigger piece of plywood, then built a bigger bank. Afterward, he grinned proudly at his newer, bigger bank and thought surely it was the perfect size.

But over the next several weeks, the boy found two coins on the sidewalk and won six coins playing marbles with friends. Then his mom and dad gave him even more coins—and even some paper money— on his birthday. The bills, the boy soon discovered, wouldn't fit through the small slot of his new wooden bank.

The boy was happy to have more coins and new crisp bills. But once again, his little treasure wouldn't all fit in his bank, and he was tired of building new banks.

Being a wise little boy, he decided to ask his father for help. His father had just the answer. The father gave the boy a big, beautiful bank of his very own. The youngster then put all his money in the new big bank: one hundred coins of various sizes and shapes and ten whole dollars. And although he had lots of room left over, the boy knew the bank that his father gave to him could get fuller and fuller without running out of room.

A parable by me: "Don't build your own bank to fit your coins."

The little boy is us.

The father is God.

The coins are our faith.

The bank is the Word of God.

Don't build your own bank to fit your coins.

Spiritual growth will be frustrating if you have to rebuild your bank—the way you understand God's Word—every time your coins increase—your faith in God enlarges. Your Father has given you the greatest bank there is—the Bible. Put your faith—your coins—in it. Your few coins—your small faith—may swim around in that big bank at first, but if you're seeking more coins—a bigger, stronger faith—they'll increase with plenty of room for growth.

Think about This

That sounds great, you're probably thinking. But how do you choose the Word of God as your bank?

1. Acknowledge that you don't have to yet have faith in something for it to be true.
2. Believe your Heavenly Father.

You don't have to have faith yet for everything in the Bible. Just read Scriptures with an open mind and heart. Each time you open your Bible to read the Word of God, say this to yourself: "The Bible says it, so it's true whether I understand it or not, whether I've seen it or not, and whether I have complete faith in it now or not."

Once, a young woman confided in me that she had created a safe "box" for God to live. Whenever she read a Scripture that she didn't understand or that didn't fit in the box she created for God, she was upset and confused.

This was one of her situations. She understood that God was always loving and that He *is* love (1 John 4:16). So how could a loving God ever send someone to hell?

First of all, she had to let God live in His Word (the Bible) instead of her box. In doing so, He can be and do all that the Word says—even when she didn't understand it all.

Then I explained to her that love is *always* a choice. God created people to love Him and have a relationship with Him. He would not be a truly loving God if He hadn't given us the choice to love Him or not love Him. Love is love only if it is a choice.

God didn't want robots forced to love Him. He wanted sons and daughters who would really love Him from their hearts only because they chose to do so. In allowing choices, God took a huge risk—after all, people were now free to reject Him.

Think about This

God *is* love and everything good is God—sunshine, friends, hugs, great times, special animals, the love between all people, and even our very existence. So separation from God, by our choice, would mean separation forever from *all* that is good and all that is love—everything that brings joy, peace, and happiness.

And because God honors our choices, if we reject Him and choose to be separated from Him on this earth, then God will honor that choice of separation for eternity. And that would be Hell.

There will always be things in the Bible that you'll have to work through. There will even be things that you never fully grasp or understand on this earth.

So put your few coins—the faith you have today in the Word of God—the best bank ever—and two great things will happen:

1. Your Faith will increase. You can count on it.
2. You will find that the Word of God is true. You can bank on it.

Pray

Lord, I acknowledge I don't have to have faith yet in something for it to be true. I choose today to believe Your Word is true, even if I may not completely have faith in all of it yet. As I trust and seek You, I desire for my faith to grow so that I can experience all of Your blessings and have abundant life. Amen.

Believe

"Through Him [Jesus Christ] you believe in God, who raised Him from the dead and glorified Him, and so your faith [coins] and hope are in God [the bank]" (1 Pet 1:21).

For Journaling and Reflection

1. Have you ever felt that something you read in the Bible didn't match up with what you understood about God and Jesus at the time? Think about that experience. Has the way you understand the Bible changed since that time? In your journal, write about how your new way of understanding has helped you.
2. The story of the little boy's bank is a kind of parable—a story that can give us a deeper perspective of our growing faith. What experience has God used in your life to grow your faith (for example, being nervous in a new setting, or resolving a conflict with a close friend)? Try using your experience to write a parable about how faith grows and how God reveals more and more to you as your faith increases.
3. Do you have to completely believe or understand something in order for it to be true? When was the last time you put your faith in something you didn't completely understand (air travel, electricity, music downloads)?

Fourteen

Where Is Your Spiritual Location?

Finding Yourself in Christ

If I asked you, "Where is your physical location?" you'd probably give me the address of the building you're in or the name of the street or highway you're on. Or you might just say the name of your city or neighborhood. And you'd most likely answer quickly and easily.

So let me now ask you another question: "Where is your spiritual location?"

You'd probably stumble over that one. It seems like a weird question, and it's not exactly an everyday conversation starter. What on earth would you say in response?

> ### Think about This
>
> A physical location is where you are in the physical realm—walking down the street, swimming in the ocean, climbing a mountain, sitting in the library.
>
> A spiritual location is where you are in the spiritual realm—far from God, close to God, or maybe somewhere in between.

In school, we study physical locations all the time when we take classes in geography, history, archeology, or astronomy. But hardly anyone considers spiritual locations.

Our society seems to have the attitude that spiritual locations don't matter. And when something isn't important we say: "It doesn't matter (have substance in the physical realm)," or "It's immaterial."

The irony is locations, even without substance, *do* matter.

Why? Think of it this way: Physical locations (the earth, the sea, mountains, and so on) were created in a spiritual location (in God).

Genesis 1:1 says that in the beginning God created the earth. God is a Spirit (2 Cor 3:17). So our physical location (earth) was created (or birthed) within the spiritual location of God.

Wow! The spiritual made the physical!

In the same way, although we were born from our mother's bodies (a physical location), the Bible tell us in Psalm 139 that we were first created in God and by God in a spiritual location (a secret place).

> My frame was not hidden from You
> when I was made in the secret place.
> When I was woven together in the depths of the earth,
>
> Your eyes saw my unformed body.
> All the days ordained for me
> were written in Your book
> before one of them came to be. (Ps 139:15–16)

Here's a brain twister: Every person who chooses Christ as Savior was created in a spiritual location (Ps 139), born in a physical location (Ps 139), reborn in spiritual location (John 3:3–6), will die in a physical location (Heb 9:27; Phil 1:21), will live forever in a spiritual location (John 3:16).

So we're spiritual beings whose spirits will live forever, temporarily dwelling in a physical location where we will leave after our bodies some-day die.

So think again about your answer to this question: "Where is your spiritual location?"

Did you know that when a person prays to receive Jesus as Savior, he or she is literally transported spiritually and reborn spiritually?

Keep these things in mind while you read Colossians 1:13–16:

> For He has rescued us from the dominion of darkness and brought us into the kingdom of the Son He loves, in Whom we have redemption, the forgiveness of sins. He is the image of the invisible God, the firstborn over all creation. For by Him all things were created: things in heaven and on earth, visible and invisible, whether thrones or powers or rulers or authorities; all things were created by Him and for Him.

Take a minute to highlight the spiritual and physical locations in this passage.

So . . . where is your spiritual location?

When you become a Christian, your spiritual location is in God's Kingdom, in God or in Christ.

> "Your life is now hidden with Christ in God" (Col 3:3).
>
> "If anyone acknowledges that Jesus is the Son of God, God lives in him and he in God" (1 John 4:15).
>
> "Whoever lives in love lives in God, and God in him" (1 John 4:16).
>
> "It is because of Him that you are in Christ Jesus" (1 Cor 1:30).
>
> "For as in Adam all die, so in Christ all will be made alive" (1 Cor 15:22).
>
> "Therefore, if anyone is in Christ, he is a new creation" (2 Cor 5:17).
>
> "And you also were included in Christ when you heard the word of truth" (Eph 1:13). "God raised us up with Christ and seated us with Him in the heavenly realms in Christ" (Eph 2:6–7).
>
> "But now in Christ Jesus you who once were far away have been brought near" (Eph 2:13).

Let's see what we can learn from these Scripture passages. Everyone today seems to be trying to "find themselves." There is a lot of soul-searching and self-analysis. People try everything from hypnosis to personality testing to journaling to analyzing their dreams. You name it.

But why? Because deep down inside almost all of us want to know who we are, why we're here, and what we're supposed to be doing.

Now here's the clincher: If you're a Christian and your life is hidden in Christ—like the Bible says—then you will not be able to completely find the real you in anything other than Jesus.

Have you ever lost a file on the computer and couldn't remember where you saved it? It's frustrating to try to find the file, especially when you can't remember what you named it or when you saved it. You have to do a search until you can find the folder you saved it in before you can open it and use it.

In pretty much the same way, the life of a Christian has been saved in Christ's file. Only in opening Him will you find *you.*

Where is *your* spiritual location?

If you're outside of Christ, you will never find who you were really created to be by God. The prayer below will bring you into His Kingdom if you really mean the words when you pray them.

Think about This

If you are already a Christian but need to know who you are, why you're here, and what you're supposed to be doing—then get ready because:

As you open Christ's file—the Bible—you'll find your awesome life!

Pray

God, I want to know who I am. I want to find my spiritual location in You. You created me and You know me. I choose now to ask You to come into my heart and forgive my wrongs. I am asking You to be my Lord—knowing now that my life located in You will be blessed and full of promise.

Father, thank you for rescuing me from the kingdom of darkness and placing me into the Kingdom of Your Son, Jesus. Please help me to find myself in Him so that I will fulfill all the good promises written about me in Your book. Amen.

Believe

"For he has rescued us from the dominion of darkness and brought us into the kingdom of the Son He loves, in whom we have redemption, the forgiveness of sins. He is the image of the invisible God, the firstborn over all creation. For by Him all things were created: things in heaven and on earth, visible and invisible, whether thrones or powers or rulers or authorities; all things were created by Him and for Him" (Col 1:13–16).

For Journaling and Reflection

1. Imagine you had a GPS—global positioning system—device that helped you track not your physical but your spiritual location. Where would it be? Write down a description of your location in your journal. Are you in a different place spiritually than you were a month ago? A year ago? Write about the ways your location may have changed and why.

2. In what locations (other than Jesus) have you searched for your identity, only to come up empty-handed (books, music, movies)?

3. How well must God know you if He knew you before you were born! But sometimes it's still hard to trust God with our secret dreams, plans, and purpose. What do you have trouble entrusting to God? Write a prayer asking God to give you the courage to trust His work in your life.

4. Have you ever been in a great physical location, but at the same time a terrible spiritual location—maybe you were at a wonderful party, but worried that no one liked you, or you were on a great vacation but spent the whole time arguing with your family. What about vice versa? Have you ever been in a terrible physical location but a great spiritual location at the same time—maybe you got lost on your way to a friend's house but didn't panic because you trusted God and knew you'd be okay, or you had a teacher who seemed to treat you unfairly but you stayed calm and showed God's love anyway. Write about one of those times, and think about how God was working in you through that experience.

Fifteen

Timing Is Everything

Putting Your Life in God's Hands

When my daughter Mattie was six years old, she decided that more than anything else in the world she wanted to drive my car. She asked daily when she could get behind the wheel.

This from a kindergartener who was only just learning to read and hadn't even mastered riding a bicycle!

One day when I picked her up from school, she asked again—as usual—when she would be driving. "Mattie," I told her, "just enjoy doing what you're doing right now, because it's going to be ten years before you can get your driver's license."

"How much is ten years?" she said leaning forward and raising one eyebrow.

"Approximately 3,650 days," I said, grateful to still be one step ahead of her, "so why keep asking and being sad about something you can't do yet or don't have yet, when you have so many things to enjoy today?" I watched her thoughtful expression in the rearview mirror.

There was silence in the back seat. And then a little voice asked boldly, "MoMy, can *you* drive me to get that rainbow ice cream that you say looks like playdough? And can I get guMy bears on top?"

Silenced up front in the driver's seat, I realized I was no longer one step ahead of her. "Okay, but in a cup, not a cone. I don't want rainbow ice cream all over my car."

Mattie may have been only six years old, but she had already discovered that waiting for the right timing can be really hard. A friend of mine told me about how she discovered this very same lesson many years ago. When she was a young girl, she and her brothers and sisters each took turns churning an old-fashioned homemade ice cream maker.

Being the oldest child, my friend always took the last turn. Her parents had told her not to stop turning the handle until the ice cream became almost impossible to churn, because that meant it was ready.

One summer day her little mouth was watering for the creamy sweetness, and she felt it really wouldn't matter if she quit a little early. So when her turn came around, she churned for a little while and then announced that the ice cream was ready. But when it was dished out it, it wasn't even ice cream—it was just mushy sweet milk. What a disappointment! What a lesson!

There's a lesson for all of us here. Don't quit too soon. Don't insist on getting something too early. Be willing to wait. *Timing is everything.*

All my life I've prayed for God's will, but only in the last several years have I prayed for God's timing.

I received an e-mail from a close friend in Israel. I had written to ask her how to say "God's timing" in Hebrew. She responded that there is no set Hebrew expression for "God's timing," but the closest phrase that is used frequently is *Ratzon Ha-El*, which means "God's will."

God's Timing = God's Will.

It took me a long time to learn, but now I understood: God's will and God's timing are pretty much the same thing.

The great news is God's will is good and perfect: "That good, and acceptable, and perfect, will of God" (Rom 12:2, KJV).

More great news is God's will is to prosper us and give us a wonderful future: "'For I know the plans I have for you,' declares the LORD, 'plans to prosper you and not to harm you, plans to give you hope and a future'" (Jer 29:11).

But after all, we're only human, and it can be really hard to understand God's timing. We know what we want when we want it. And feel that we know what is best for all. So sometimes it seems that God's timing is way off.

Recently, a precious friend of mine felt God's timing was too soon because she didn't plan on having a baby right after she got married. But it turned out to be perfect timing—a perfect baby and God's perfect will.

But for most of us, most of the time, God's timing doesn't seem to be too early, but instead, too late. Another dear friend had had a brain tumor for more than four years before her doctors figured out exactly what was wrong with her. By the time the tumor was found, the outlook was very bleak. But she told me that she and her husband wouldn't have their adorable four-year-old child if God had revealed the situation earlier, because she would not have tried to become pregnant. And today, she is so thankful to have both her life and her little girl.

What in your life today seems too soon? Or what in your life today seems too late?

> ### Think about This
>
> God's timing is God's will.
>   God's will is perfect and good. So God's timing is perfect and good.

Driving too soon could be a giant disaster. Unfinished ice cream tastes like mushy milk. And most important: The *really* significant things in life—our futures, our relationships, our plans—will only be prosperous with God's perfect timing.

When we put our lives *in* God's hands, then our families, our health, our money, our relationships, and our dreams are in His perfect timing. But when we take these things *out* of God's hands and try to control them ourselves—then we can get way *out* of God's timing and usually way *in* trouble.

So what do we do?

Maybe something seems to have happened too soon in your life—for instance if your parents are having financial problems, you may have to get a job and take on more responsibility earlier than most kids your age. Or maybe something doesn't seem to be happening soon enough—your parents might not let you go out on a date yet even though many of your friends can. Trust God anyway! Be determined to enjoy what you have today, and wait for what is to come—in God's perfect timing.

Remember this: God's timing will be His perfect will. And His perfect will is better than you can even imagine.

> Now to Him who is able to do immeasurably more than all we ask or imagine, according to His power that is at work within us. (Eph 3:20)

Pray

Dear Jesus, I pray for Your perfect timing and Your perfect will in every area of my life, knowing Your will for me is good, prosperous, and the best plan for me.

God, please help me to trust You with the things that seem too early or too late. Forgive me for not trusting You with some things that have seemed too soon and for not enjoying what You have given me today because of something I want in the future.

I know Your will and Your timing are perfect, and I want nothing less than Your best for me. Thank You for Your love and patience. Thank You for Your good plan for my life—the blessings I've received from You and the blessings yet to come. Amen.

Believe

"... Do not be conformed to this world but be transformed by the renewing of your mind that you may prove what the will of God is, that which is good, acceptable and perfect" (Rom 12:2, NAS).

"'For I know the plans I have for you,' declares the LORD, 'plans to prosper you and not to harm you, plans to give you hope and a future'" (Jer 29:11).

For Journaling and Reflection

1. Are you eager for one phase of your life to end and another to begin? Maybe you're looking forward to high school graduation or to finishing your last college course and finally getting out into the world. Instead of wishing today away, think of three things to gratefully participate in during this phase of your life.

2. Look at God's promise for you in Jeremiah 29:11. Is that particular promise easy to take personally, accept, and believe? Why or why not?

3. If God's timing and God's will are pretty much the same thing, consider the circumstances in your life. How does that take the pressure off *you* to fix things, rush things, explain things, or make sense of them?

Sixteen

Are We a Nike Generation?

Displaying the Fruit of Spirit

> "In this world you will have trouble. But take heart! I have overcome the world." (John 16:33)

The word "trouble" in John 16:33 is translated from the Greek word *yliqiv,*which implies a pressing together or pressure. The root word for *yliqiv* is *ylibw*, which means "to press as grapes." When grapes or any fruit are pressed, then the true contents of the fruit comes out.

Recently, I purchased some beautiful, firm, healthy green limes. When I placed them among the apples and bananas, they brightened up the whole fruit bowl. But when I tried to squeeze the limes into my iced tea, I was very disappointed. The healthy, beautiful appearance of the limes was deceiving. They hardly gave any juice—they were beautiful, but they were dry.

I thought about those picture-perfect limes the other day when I began to eat a grapefruit that was advertised as juicy and sweet. It was juicy all right, but it was so sour that I couldn't help but make that puckered-up face that's the international symbol for "Yuck!"

Squeezing all this bad fruit prompted me to think about the phrase "putting the squeeze on." It's used when someone is under a lot of pressure. Whether it's news events, a world crisis, or trouble in our personal lives, everybody feels pressure. But do you know that what comes out of you while you're under pressure is what's really inside of you?

If you're a Christian, then the Holy Spirit is living inside of you and what comes out of you—in easy times and tough times—should be the fruit of the Spirit.

What is this fruit exactly? Galatians 5:22–23 tells us that "the fruit of the Spirit is love, joy, peace, patience, kindness, goodness, faithfulness, gentleness, and self-control."

But fruit is proven only in testing. In other words, only after you squeeze a fruit can you really know what's inside.

In much the same way, only after trouble and pressure squeeze us is our spiritual fruit revealed. Faith can look bright, shiny, and beautiful on the outside, but when a time of testing brings pressures into our lives, some people's faith turns out to be sour, or even completely dry (nonexistent).

In Luke 8:13 Jesus says that some will "receive the word with joy when they hear it, but they have no root. They believe for a while, but in the time of testing they fall away."

Think about This

"Check the Root to Have Good Fruit"
The root of our faith
needs to be the very core belief
that God loves us,
we can trust Him,
and we will ultimately be victorious
in all things through Him.

"In this world you will have trouble [you will be squeezed as grapes]. But take heart! I have overcome the world." (John 16:33)

The word "overcome" in John 16:33 is expressed by the Greek word *nikaw*, which means "to prevail, to conquer, and to carry off the victory." *Nikaw* also is the root of the word *nike*, which means victory.

Is Nike a familiar word to you? Think tennis shoes and work-out gear. A recent advertising campaign for Nike called us the "Nike Generation." Are we? Are we a victorious generation?

Spiritually speaking, if I don't have the root or core belief—that God loves me, that I can trust Him, and that I'll ultimately be victorious in all things through Him—then when pressure comes, I probably won't be able to pour forth the fruit of the Spirit: love, joy, peace, patience, kindness, goodness, faithfulness, gentleness, and self-control. For example, if I have the core belief that God doesn't really love or care about me, then when the difficult circumstances of life give me "the squeeze," I will probably exhibit the fruit of fear instead of peace and the fruit of panic instead of patience.

Another scenario: I might exhibit a very sour attitude toward life, but excuse it by saying that I had been under a lot of pressure. Believers of all spiritual maturity levels tend to use times of testing (pressure) as an excuse for bad fruit instead of an opportunity to exhibit the fruit of the Spirit. Somebody might excuse their bad behavior, for instance, with an announcement like this one: "Well, the reason I bit your head off on the phone is because my fiancé just called off the wedding and started dating someone else!"

We all make mistakes, but God is looking for a generation who will display the fruit of the Spirit—love, joy, peace, patience, kindness, goodness, faithfulness, gentleness, and self-control—even when we're squeezed. Especially when we're squeezed.

> This is how we know that we love the children of God: by loving God and carrying out His commands. This is love for God: to obey His commands. And His commands are not burdensome, for everyone born of God overcomes the world. This is the victory that has overcome the world, even our faith. (1 John 5:2–4)

Pray

Dear Jesus, I can think of times when I was pressured or squeezed and I didn't exhibit the fruit of the Spirit of love, joy, peace, patience, kindness, goodness, faithfulness, gentleness, and self-control. As a matter of fact, my attitude was sour and my faith seemed dry.

God please forgive me and give me the grace to develop a deep root in knowing that You love me, I can trust You, and I will ultimately be victorious in all things through You so I will have the right fruit.

Please put me with people who will encourage this core belief. I want to be a part of Your Nike/victorious generation. Amen.

Believe

"In this world you will have trouble. But take heart! I have overcome the world" (John 16:33).

"The fruit of the Spirit is love, joy, peace, patience, kindness, goodness, faithfulness, gentleness, and self-control" (Gal 5:22–23).

Jesus says that some will "receive the word with joy when they hear it, but they have no root. They believe for a while, but in the time of testing they fall away" (Luke 8:13).

"This is how we know that we love the children of God: by loving God and carrying out His commands. This is love for God: to obey His commands. And His commands are not burdensome, for everyone born of God overcomes the world. This is the victory that has overcome the world, even our faith" (1 John 5:2–4).

For Journaling and Reflection

1. If someone put the squeeze on you right now, what kind of juice would come out? Would it be sweet (love, joy, peace, patience, kindness, goodness, faithfulness, gentleness, self-control)? Or would it be sour (anger, bitterness, impatience, unforgiveness, frustration, fear)?

2. Those sweet juices in the previous question are the fruit of the Spirit. Probably some of them come easier to you than others. Which comes easiest? Which one seems to be the hardest for you?

3. Have you ever been surprised by your own reaction when you got squeezed—either by exhibiting the fruit of the Spirit when you could have gotten upset or by losing your patience with someone when they perhaps did not deserve it? Think about ways you can exhibit the fruit of the Spirit in your life this week.

Seventeen

No Regrets

Living a Life of Belief, Forgiveness, and Love

Years ago, I was diagnosed with a kind of cancer called leukemia. A lot goes through a person's mind when something like that happens. One of the things that many people think about is regrets.

A long time ago I decided I wanted to live a life of no regrets. Like everyone, I have things in my life I've said wrong, done wrong, and thought wrong. But thankfully, God offers all of us the opportunity to live a life of no regrets. How?

First, we must believe Romans 8:28 is true—that all things work for good for those who love God and are called according to His purpose. God is telling us He will even turn our mistakes into good if we love Him and have chosen to belong to Him.

One young person who came from a difficult home life once forcefully stated, "My parents should have never married."

I waited for a minute before asking her, "Are you adopted?"

"No," she replied.

"Well, I'm glad you're here," I said. A slow grin spread across her face as she realized that without her parent's "mistaken relationship" she wouldn't even exist.

If we believe and trust God, then we can know for sure He'll take every mistake, every sin, and every mess and work it for our good.

Second, to live a life of no regrets we must receive God's forgiveness. And after He forgives us, we need to forgive ourselves and others.

I believe the mistakes I've made—and there are too many to count—can either be stepping stones or stumbling blocks in my life. If I don't ask God to forgive me, receive that forgiveness, and forgive myself and others, then that mess will forever be a stumbling block in my life. It will trip me up in other relationships, cause me further pain, and keep me from walking in the path that God calls me to walk.

But if I forgive and receive forgiveness, then the mistake I've made or the mess I've gotten myself into can become a stepping-stone in my life. It can help me realize what I've done wrong and how I need to change. A stepping-stone can be sharp or even slippery, but when you're hiking to higher ground, then that stepping-stone becomes the platform that moves you to a higher place.

True Christians want to walk in the ways of God and glorify Him with their lives. So turning troubles into stepping stones helps us move to a better place spiritually, and that makes us more able to love, forgive, and walk out this life following God's amazingly good path.

I recently heard somebody say: "We enjoy in the good times what we learned in the hard times." I believe that's so true! We build success on the strong foundation of what we've learned from our failures and pain.

Think about This

What mistakes have you made? Do you believe God can work them for good in your life? Have you received His forgiveness for your mistakes? Have you forgiven yourself and others?

Do you view these mistakes as stumbling blocks or stepping-stones?

No regrets also means living and loving God's way. What is God's way?

> "Love the Lord your God with all your heart and with all your soul and with all your mind." This is the first and greatest commandment. And the second is like it: "Love your neighbor as yourself." (Matt 22:37–39)

God's greatest commandment isn't: "Figure out the right answers to everything." When we go to heaven, Jesus isn't going to say, "Your interpretation of Scriptures was really off." Instead, we hope and pray He welcomes us with words like these: "Well done good and faithful servant. You loved the Lord your God with all your heart, and with all your soul, and with all your mind, and you loved your neighbor as yourself."

So put first things first. When my young daughter goes to bed, I tell her to do two things: put on her pajamas and brush her teeth. I'm not pleased when I go into her room to read her a story and discover that she's colored a picture, picked a half-eaten lollipop out of the sock she hid it in, brushed her doll's hair, and arranged a line of stuffed animals across the bed.

I ask her: "Did you do the two things I asked you to do?"

And she says, "No, but I picked the candy out of my sock, moved my stuffed animals, brushed my doll's hair, and colored."

And although these may be perfectly good things to do, I'm not pleased, because she left undone the two important things I told her to do first.

My young daughter approaches bedtime the same way many of us approach our spiritual lives. We may try to do many things for God, but leave undone the few things that He asked us to do first.

> "Many will say to Me on that day, 'Lord, Lord, did we not prophesy in Your name, and in Your name drive out demons and perform many miracles?' Then I will tell them plainly, 'I never knew you. Away from Me, you evildoers!'" (Matt 7:22–23)

It's so easy to put a lot of other good activities in the place of our Father's two most important things—loving God and others. It's also easy to feel that because we're not doing bad things like gossiping, taking drugs, lying, cheating, or stealing, we're doing the right things.

Thinking about this might give us a different picture of this Scripture passage:

> Enter through the narrow gate. For wide is the gate and broad is the road that leads to destruction, and many enter through it. But small is the gate and narrow the road that leads to life, and only a few find it. (Matt 7:13–14)

The wide road is a lot like my daughter's room. There are so many other things to do besides the few things I've told her to do.

Think of it this way: The wide road could be the whole highway of life and the narrow road could be the main lane of loving God and loving others. The tough thing about staying in the main lane is that there are so many other lanes, both good and bad, that we can move over and drive in.

But a life of no regrets means we love the Lord our God with all our hearts and with all our souls and with all our minds, and we love our neighbor as ourselves before we even think about changing lanes.

A life of no regrets means putting first things first.

How do we choose to love God and love others?

Some of the dearest reflections of my life are the times when I have taken the opportunity to love others. When my daughter was two, I told her I loved her, and we could do anything she wanted to do that afternoon. She sat in her car seat swinging her little pudgy two-year-old legs while she was thinking. Finally she said, "I wanna go home and make some bacon."

"Bacon?" I questioned. "Did you say you want to go home and make bacon?"

"Yep," she nodded. And we did. We ate bacon together, and my daughter felt loved.

When we go to Heaven, God won't ask us what committee we chaired, what Bible study we ran, or what religious argument we won. God will ask us if we loved.

Living a life of no regrets isn't a complicated life but a life that seizes the opportunity to love others. And many times it's much easier to love strangers than our own families.

Loving others means calling the lonely relative who is always crabby but needs patience and attention. Loving others means not having to win the argument with our parents. Loving others can mean fishing with little brother, even if you hate worms, because it's a good time to talk. Loving others can mean shopping for just the right shade of lip gloss with your good friend if it means something to her. Loving others can mean spending time with your grandparents when you could be with your friends. Loving others can even mean eating bacon with a two-year-old.

And finally, no regrets not only means loving others, but most importantly it means loving God and His Son.

When I was in the hospital I became friends with a nurse I'll call Lee (his name has been changed). Because of his beard and tattoos, Lee might've first appeared to be a rough character, but he had a heart of gold. He was a new daddy, so proud of his little boy, and every day he showed me pictures and told me stories of the latest things his son was doing.

Lee saw me studying my Bible one day. "I see you reading the Bible and listening to God songs and praying and stuff, and I have a question," Lee said, nearing the foot of my bed.

"Shoot," I said, putting down my pen.

"Okay, I believe in God and everything, and there is even enough historical evidence to where I believe Jesus is God's Son. But here's the deal: Why do you have to believe in Jesus and 'accept Him' to get to God? Why do I have to ask Jesus into my heart, too?"

My heart quickened as God gave me the answer for Lee.

"Lee, imagine I invited you over to my house, and you brought your son. When I met you at my door I greeted you and told you to come in, but I told you your son had to wait outside, that he was not welcome. What would you say?"

Without hesitation Lee said, "I would have to say if my son is not welcome then I am not welcome either."

I choked on the next words, seeing the beautiful picture God had orchestrated just for Lee. "That's what God said, Lee. That's what God said. If my Son is not welcome, then I am not either."

The next few minutes were a miraculous whirlwind as Lee bowed his head and asked Jesus to come into his heart. And although it had nothing to do with me, I realized that choosing to love God with all my heart and soul and mind had not only made my life a life of no regrets, but it had touched the life of another.

Pray

Dear God, I want to live a life of no regrets. Please forgive me for my mistakes, my sins, and my messes.

Please forgive me specifically for _____. With God's help, I choose to forgive myself for _____. With God's help, I choose to forgive others for _____.

God, please use every mistake I've made, and every sin I've committed, and every mess I've created, and every hurt I've endured as a stepping stone to bring me to a higher place with You.

Father, teach me to love You and to love others. Show me how to better love my own family and those nearest to me. Show me how I can love others not only through You, but to You. In Jesus' Name, Amen.

Believe

"All things work for good for those who love God and are called according to His purpose" (Rom 8:28).

"'Love the Lord your God with all your heart and with all your soul and with all your mind.' This is the first and greatest commandment. And the second is like it: 'Love your neighbor as yourself'" (Matt 22:37–39).

"Many will say to Me on that day, 'Lord, Lord, did we not prophesy in Your name, and in Your name drive out demons and perform many miracles?' Then I will tell them plainly, 'I never knew you. Away from Me, you evildoers!'" (Matt 7:22–23).

"Enter through the narrow gate. For wide is the gate and broad is the road that leads to destruction, and many enter through it. But small is the gate and narrow the road that leads to life, and only a few find it" (Matt 7:13–14).

For Journaling and Reflection

1. Think of a mistake in your life that you haven't let go of and no matter what you tried, you haven't been able to fix it yourself. If you continue to try to fix it yourself, that old mistake could remain a stumbling block—you might assume the worst without knowing the facts, repeat the mistake, or just keep living with ongoing guilt. In what ways could stepping back and letting God transform your mistake into a stepping-stone turn things around for you? (For example, you might be able to help someone with the same problem or avoid the same mistake, or you might even help to repair broken relationship.)

2. What sort of things might you do—that aren't necessarily bad—that turn your focus away from loving God and your neighbor as yourself?

3. The gate is small and the way is narrow (Matt 7:13–14), so that can explain why not everyone in the crowd is following God. When is living God's truth hardest for you? When is living God's truth easiest for you?

Eighteen

Faithful

Appreciating Faithfulness

I've been thinking about the word "faithful" and about all the faithful people in my life.

Faithful people aren't necessarily the ones who shine. And they aren't necessarily the ones with whom I always agree. The faithful people in my life are the ones who loved me and stuck around no matter what.

Faithfulness makes me think about my parents. My parents were there to take care of me as an infant. My parents were there when I went through all my ups and downs at school. My parents were there at my wedding, the birth of my daughter, the adoption of my son, and all my many joys and an assortment of traumas.

They weren't, I admit, always my favorite people—especially when I was a teenager. There were plenty of other people I liked a whole lot better. Others who seemed more in line with my personality. Others who seemed more right. Others who even seemed more important.

But *others* didn't always turn out to be faithful. And to this day, as those *others* have come and gone, my parents are still there, still faithful.

Life's difficult circumstances may have prevented one or even both of your parents from being faithful persons in your life. But God will usually prompt others to be faithful to you.

Think about This

Stop a moment and reflect on the faithful people in your life.
Have you ever slowed down to appreciate them?

> Have you ever thanked them?
>   Not because they're perfect
>   Not because they're always right
>   But because they are *faithful*.

Faithfulness makes me think about the quiet people who love and serve God. They aren't necessarily the spotlight people. They aren't necessarily the people who shine brightly, but they are the people who show up.

A lot of Christians are like Halley's Comet, appearing once every seventy-six years with lots of hoopla. Everyone makes a big deal because its appearance is flashy and important.

But faithful Christians are like the night stars, consistently showing up every night. They're easy to ignore unless you make up your mind to notice and appreciate their beauty.

God's faithful people are the ones who pray for years, having faith in God until they see His answer come forth. God's faithful people minister to the sick, spend hours alone in prayer, and study so that they can teach His Word to others, change diapers in the nursery, work in the soup kitchen, help clean up after everyone else has gone, aid the lonely and poor, build shelter for the homeless, and do all they can to glorify God and help others.

Faithfulness is so important to God. In the end God won't say: "Well done good and exciting servant," or "Well done good-looking servant," or "Well done good and popular servant." No. To all those who have been faithful He will say, "Well done good and *faithful* servant."

"Faithful" in the New Testament is expressed by the Greek word *pistos* (pis-tos') meaning "trusty, believing, and one who is worthy of trust."

"Faithful" in the Old Testament is expressed by the Hebrew word *'aman* (aw-man') meaning "to support, confirm, and be faithful." This Hebrew word is where we get our word "amen," which means "verily, truly, so be it."

The word "amen" is a most remarkable word. It was transliterated directly from the Hebrew language into the Greek language of the New Testament, then into Latin and into English and many other languages, so that's why it is practically a universal word. It's the same in almost any language.

"Amen" has been called the most recognized and most familiar word in human speech. And it's directly related—almost identical—to the

Hebrew word for believe (*amam*), or faithful. Thus, it has evolved to mean "sure or truly" (#543, "amen," *Strong's Hebrew and Greek Concordance*, from Hebrew and Chaldee Dictionary, 14), an expression of absolute "trust and confidence"(#281, "amēn," *Strong's Hebrew and Greek Concordance*, from Greek Dictionary of the New Testament, 10).

Amen can be used at the beginning of a statement or at the end. When amen is used at the beginning of a statement, it means surely, verily, or truly. When we use amen at the end of a statement or prayer, it means so be it or may it be fulfilled.

So the word amen reminds us of Jesus. Jesus is the Alpha and the Omega—the Beginning and the End.

Jesus is faithful. Whether you knew it or not, Jesus was there at the beginning of your life. He is with you *now*, and He will remain with you forever.

When all others disappoint you or even walk out on you, Jesus will remain. Jesus is the most faithful.

Pray

Dear God, please teach me to be faithful in the things You've given me to do. Please forgive me for the times I haven't been faithful and the times I've complained.

Please show me the people in my life who I need to pray for faithfully. I know I can't pray for everyone, so I'm relying on You to let me know each day. Please show me the people who I am to visit and the ministries I am to be faithful to help. I want to be counted as one of Your faithful.

Lord, please show me ways I can demonstrate faithfulness to my family so that my generation and even future generations might be faithful as well.

God, I am also asking You to open my eyes to the faithful people around me. I've taken it for granted that they'll always be there. Please reveal ways for me to express my sincere appreciation to them.

Jesus, please bless the faithful people who may never be thanked by anyone on this earth: those who care for the elderly, the mentally challenged, or anyone in difficult, even life-threatening situations who remain faithful to You and Your Word.

I pray especially for missionaries who are persecuted and imprisoned for faithfully serving You in communities that are hostile to Your Word. God, please protect and deliver Your people. Thank You for Your promise to reward them, because You are faithful. And thank You, Lord, that You will have the last word, for You are the "Amen."

Believe

"Many a man claims to have unfailing love, but a faithful man who can find?" (Prov 20:6).

"His master replied, 'Well done, good and faithful servant! You have been faithful with a few things; I will put you in charge of many things. Come and share your master's happiness!'" (Matt 25:23).

"Let us hold unswervingly to the hope we profess, for He who promised is faithful" (Heb 10:23).

"They will make war against the Lamb, but the Lamb will overcome them because He is Lord of lords and King of kings—and with Him will be His called, chosen and faithful followers"(Rev 17:14).

"I Am the Alpha and the Omega," says the Lord God, "Who is, and Who was, and Who is to come, the Almighty" (Rev 1:8).

"I Am the Alpha and the Omega, the First and the Last, the Beginning and the End" (Rev 22:13).

For Journaling and Reflection

1. Who are the people in your life who have been faithful to you no matter what? How do they show their faithfulness? What is it about their faithfulness that you appreciate the most?

2. Do you know a faithful person who might not ever get thanked or appreciated? Make a point to thank them for what they do. Write them a note or send them an e-mail. Ask God to show what to say.

3. Are you aware of it when your faith falters in yourself, in others, in God? Are you hard on yourself when that happens? Talk to God about receiving His forgiveness and ask Him to show you where He needs you most.

4. Have there been times in your life when "others" turned out to NOT be so faithful? Who did you turn to for comfort, understanding, encouragement? This was probably someone who is truly faithful to you. What do these people show you, through their lives, about the faithfulness of God?

Nineteen

Caller ID

Recognizing God's Voice

What do you think of when I say "phone solicitor," "prank caller," or even "phone scam"?

For me, the first thing that comes to mind is: "Thank goodness for caller ID."

Maybe you don't remember, but not so long ago we had to answer every call because there was no way to tell who was calling. Now phone numbers appear on a display so we don't have to answer every call in order to see who is calling.

All of us receive phone calls at inconvenient times and sometimes from unwelcome sources. Of course we shouldn't be rude to people who are trying to make an honest living by selling something over the phone. But there are calls that are best left unanswered.

Let me connect something spiritual here. In the Old Testament days, there was no caller ID. Because the enemy (satan) is not clearly identified until the New Testament, everything—good and bad—was viewed as coming from God.

If you look through your Bible, you'll see that satan is barely mentioned in the Old Testament. Jesus is the One who taught us to identify the devil.

Jesus gave us spiritual caller ID.

Jesus taught us in John 10:10 that the thief (satan) comes to kill, steal, and destroy, but Jesus came to give us life and life abundantly.

One of satan's favorite tricks is to send us thoughts, ideas, and imaginings that would have bad consequences in our lives. Satan is the oldest solicitor in the book. He's not only a prankster and a scammer, but a terrorist and a murderer—and when he shows up on our caller ID, we should never answer his call!

How can we tell if a thought is coming from satan?

Jesus shows us how. Jesus identifies the devil in many Scriptures. Here are a few:

> "He was a murderer from the beginning, not holding to the truth, for there is no truth in him. When he lies, he speaks his native language, for he is a liar and the father of lies" (John 8:44).
>
> *He lies.* He brings confusion, chaos, and critical, negative thoughts.
>
> "The thief comes only to steal and kill and destroy" (John 10:10).
>
> *He brings destruction.* He brings strife, depression, substance abuse, and destruction to relationships, friendships, futures.

Think about This

Once we've identified a thought is from the enemy, then what do we do? That's easy: Don't accept the call. Don't answer.

Jesus tells us to "take captive every thought to make it obedient to Christ" (2 Cor 10:5).

In other words, hang up on the devil!

When we get thoughts of jealousy or fear or gossip or hate or lies, then we need to ID that thought and then *reject* it. We need to get in a habit of taking every thought captive to God's ID program.

Other ways to ID the devil and the lying thoughts he sends to you:

If the thought is:

1. Contrary to Scripture, then don't answer it.
2. Not love, then let it go. (God is love; satan is fear and hate and negative things.)

3. If the image is contrary to God's good plan for your life, then hang up.

Be on the alert to ID thoughts at all times. Here are specific thoughts to hang up on:

+   Past memories that drudge up pain
+   Unforgiving or malicious feelings
+   Tormenting thoughts
+   Something that tells you to worry
+   Images of failure or rejection
+   Fearful or dreadful thoughts

Ring a bell? Next time, don't answer the ring.

We can take thoughts or we can reject thoughts just as we can take calls or we can reject calls.

God clearly tells us there are some thoughts we shouldn't take. Six times in Matthew 6 (KJV) Jesus says, "Take no thought." Each time the thought is a worry thought—what do we wear, what do we do, what shall we eat? Satan loves to send us worry thoughts because it keeps us from trusting God and from seeking Him first.

Consider this Scripture passage:

> "Therefore I say unto you, Take no thought for your life, what ye shall eat, or what ye shall drink; nor yet for your body, what ye shall put on. Is not the life more than meat, and the body than raiment? Behold the fowls of the air: for they sow not, neither do they reap, nor gather into barns; yet your heavenly Father feedeth them. Are ye not much better than they? Which of you by taking thought can add one cubit unto his stature? And why take ye thought for raiment? Consider the lilies of the field, how they grow; they toil not, neither do they spin: And yet I say unto you, That even Solomon in all his glory was not arrayed like one of these. Wherefore, if God so clothes the grass of the field, which today is, and tomorrow is cast

into the oven, shall He not much more clothe you, O ye of little faith? Therefore take no thought, saying, What shall we eat? or, What shall we drink? or, Wherewithal shall we be clothed? [For after all these things do the Gentiles seek:] for your heavenly Father knoweth that ye have need of all these things. But seek ye first the Kingdom of God, and His righteousness; and all these things shall be added unto you." (Matt 6:25–33, KJV)

Isn't it interesting that Jesus says over and over "take no thought" and then at the end of His statement says, "But seek ye first the Kingdom of God, and His righteousness."

So when it comes to those worrying thoughts, just hang up. But always be ready to pick up thoughts on God's Kingdom and righteousness.

Think about This

Have you ever had trouble "seeking first the kingdom of God?" Perhaps it's because you're taking the wrong thoughts. If we ask Him to, God will help you and me to change our thought life. It's a choice He'll give us the grace to change. The reward is great because it frees up our minds to seek His Kingdom and righteousness, and then all other things will be added unto us.

Pray

Dear Jesus, please help me to identify all the thoughts that aren't from You. Please give me Your grace and strength to hang up on these thoughts no matter how enticing it would be to answer and think about them.

Some thoughts that have gone through my mind I don't like are: _____, _____, _____, _____, _____, and _____. Please forgive me and help me to identify the thoughts coming from You versus the thoughts I should not answer.

Let me be "strong in the Lord and the power of His might" (Eph 6:10, KJV) so I might seek first Your Kingdom and righteousness. Help me clear the field of my mind so the seed of Your Word will be planted deeply and the harvest of Your perfect will will be great in my life. Amen.

Believe

Pick a Scripture from the ones mentioned in the devotion that best speaks to your heart and meditate on it. Write down the significance it has concerning your life.

For Journaling and Reflection

1. In the last twenty-four hours, when was the last time you took a call from the devil in the form of fear, unforgiveness, worry, or confusion?
2. Have you noticed satan using one particular trick on you over and over again because he always has success with it? Now that you recognize his call, how will you be ready next time to not "give him a thought"?
3. Look up Matthew 4:1–11 in your Bible and read about Jesus' conversation with satan. Where did Jesus get the words He used to "hang up" on satan and to ultimately "reject his call"? What does that teach you about how to deal with satan?

Twenty

God's Kind of Love
Unconditional and Unending

I recently skimmed an article describing the divorce between an actor and an actress. The actor was quoted as saying to his wife, "I love you; I'm just not in love with you any more."

For some reason, I've been thinking a lot about that statement. To me it means, "I love you deep down inside, but the feelings that used to make me feel good are no longer there."

As humans, we all in some way can understand the statement, "I love you; I'm just not in love with you any more." Throughout our lives, there are not only people but also events, hobbies, sports, and interests we once loved but grew tired of or less passionate about.

But was that really love in the first place?

I've seen a lot of advice columns about the difference between love and lust. But what about the difference between God's kind of love and human love?

Humanity's kind of love says, "I'll love you while you're still beautiful and make me feel good." But God's kind of love says, "I love you, and you are beautiful through the eyes of love."

Sometimes we can experience God's kind of love through a person. Two years ago my hair was falling out slowly and painfully during chemotherapy, so I asked my hairdresser to shave it all off. I never considered myself attached to my hair, but having no hair can initially make you feel naked, uncovered, and even a little shameful.

My mother and several nurses had already seen me bald. But that evening my husband, Lacey (who has known me for more than twenty years), was going to come to the hospital to see me for the first time without hair.

I thought:

If he is sad, then I will be sad.

If he looks away, I will cry.

If he ignores that my hair is gone, then I will know I repulse him.

But when Lacey walked in the room, his eyes lit up with God's kind of love, and he gave me a hug and said, "I love you without hair! It's the first time I've ever noticed your beautiful bone structure."

I learned that day God's kind of love is so deep and so true it's unveiled in layers. When one layer or aspect of human love is removed, it offers an opportunity for a deeper, truer revelation of God's love to be unveiled.

Sometimes God shows us this deeper unveiling of His love through others, but other times God's kind of love is revealed when we don't receive it from another person.

Human love says, "I'll love you while I agree with you, and as long as you please me." But God's kind of love says, "I love you, and it has nothing to do with what you do."

Have you ever been so hurt, rejected, or misunderstood that all human voices sounded like the clanging gongs mentioned in 1 Corinthians 13:1? Finally, you came to the realization only God could fully offer you the unconditional, unending love that you need.

Have you ever been so grieved, desperate, confused, or sad that you actually found strange comfort in the book of Job and finally understood God's kind of love would be the only balm to heal your wounds?

When no one else understood, look at what King David wrote about God's kind of love:

> You number my wanderings; Put my tears into Your bottle; Are they not in Your book? When I cry out to You, then my enemies turn back in the day that I call; this I know, that God is for me. In God [I will praise His Word], In Jehovah [I will praise His Word], In God have I put my trust, I will not be afraid. What can man do unto me? (Ps 56:8–11, NKJV)

Sometimes we have glimpses of God's kind of love in our lives when others truly love us in God's way, seeing us through the eyes of love. Other times, God allows an unveiling of His love when we realize no one can possibly understand or love us the exact way we need to be loved—all the time—except God.

During those times, God reaches out to us. He wants us to run into His open arms and receive the indescribable and perfect love He has for us—not because we always please Him or do the right things, but because He loves us.

Pray

Dear Jesus, please continue to reveal Your constant, perfect, and wonderful love toward me. I really need You in my life, especially concerning _____ where I do not feel loved (understood, appreciated, or cared for). I know only You can truly meet the need for love I have in my heart. Thank You for loving me forever and always and for seeing me as beautiful through Your eyes of love.

Also God, remind me of the times You have used another person to give me glimpses of Your God kind of love. Please allow me to be this person in the lives of others. Only through You can I love in Your way. Help me to love others with God's kind of love. Amen.

Believe

"You number my wanderings; Put my tears into Your bottle; Are they not in Your book? When I cry out to You, then my enemies turn back in the day that I call; This I know, that God is for me. In God [I will praise His Word], In Jehovah [I will praise His Word], In God have I put my trust, I will not be afraid. What can man do unto me?" (Ps 56:8–11, NKJV).

For Journaling and Reflection

1. Has God ever surprised you with someone's unconditional love when you were feeling or acting unlovable?
2. Has God ever moved you to be unconditionally loving toward someone who was feeling or acting unlovable?
3. Think about some of popular movies or advertisements in fashion magazines. What messages are they sending about your worthiness to be loved? Look at 1 Corinthians 13:1–9 and think about the ways God's love for you is totally different.

Twenty-one

Be Still

Stopping, Waiting, and Watching God Work

Several years ago, I was working on reading and spelling with my six-year-old daughter. Not captivated by my sage instruction, she wiggled nonstop. I must have told her to "be still" fifteen times.

She stood up and down, rocked in her chair, tapped her pencil on the desk, leaned to the left until she nearly toppled, leaned to the right until she nearly fell out of her chair, and then shook her head from side to side faster and faster until her eyes were almost crossed.

"Be still," I repeated with more and more force.

Finally, she tipped back her chair and inquired, "Why do I have to be still?"

I wondered if her childish mind could not yet comprehend that most people can't learn, listen, or focus unless they are somewhat still. I have important things to teach her that she'll really need to know, I reasoned, so I have to convince her to be still long enough to learn. "Mattie," I said in my firmest Mommy-Teacher voice, "You have to be still in order to get what I am saying!"

"Oh, well, just remind me," she replied, flapping her arms like a bird.

Do you know the funny thing? As frustrated as her reply made me, I realized God has to remind me to "be still" just like I have to remind Mattie. In my own way, I get just as fidgety and distracted as she does. Consider these Scripture passages:

- "*Be still* and know that I am God" (Ps 46:10).
- "You need only to *be still*" (Exod 14:14).
- Nehemiah 8:11 tells the people to "*Be still.*"
- "Cease and *be still*" (Jer 47:6).

- Zechariah 2:13 says, "*Be still* before the LORD, all mankind."
- Jesus even calmed the storm in Mark 4:39 by saying, "Quiet! *Be still!*"
- And finally Psalm 37:7 says for us to "*Be still* before the LORD and wait patiently for Him."

Do you think God is trying to make a point here?

Let's read a little more of Psalm 37 because God gives us specific things to do and specific things not to do—even while being still.

> "Do not fret because of evil men or be envious of those who do wrong; for like the grass they will soon wither, like green plants they will soon die away. Trust in the LORD and do good; dwell in the land and enjoy safe pasture. Delight yourself in the LORD and He will give you the desires of your heart. Commit your way to the LORD; trust in Him and He will do this: He will make your righteousness shine like the dawn, the justice of your cause like the noonday sun. Be still before the LORD and wait patiently for Him; do not fret when men succeed in their ways, when they carry out their wicked schemes. Refrain from anger and turn from wrath; do not fret—it leads only to evil. For evil men will be cut off, but those who hope in the LORD will inherit the land" (Ps 37:1–9).

Think about This

While being still we are *not* to:
    fret, fret, fret, or be angry or wrathful.
    While being still we *are* to:
    trust in the Lord, do good, delight ourselves in Him, commit our ways to Him, wait patiently for God, and hope in Him.

And notice what God promises when we do these things. When we are still and trust in the Lord, do good, delight ourselves in Him, commit our ways to Him, wait patiently for God, and hope in Him, God promises He will give us safe pasture, give us the desires of our hearts, make our righteousness shine like the dawn, and the justice of our causes like the noonday sun, and we will inherit the land. Wow! We should be still more often.

There's a time to prepare, talk, pray, reason, seek counsel, and even do battle. But there is also a time to be still.

Could it be that the answers to our prayers have been given, but we have been too "wiggly" to hear?

Could it be that God is waiting patiently for us to stop and be still before He can reveal more wonderful spiritual things?

Maybe we need a major miracle in the area of relationships or school or health, and God is simply asking us to be still and let Him do His thing. Most of us can recite Psalm 46:10, "Be still and know that I am God." But have we understood it as "Be still and know that I *am* God?" In other words, God is saying: not you—but ME—the Creator of the universe, the King of Kings, your Lord and Savior—will bring truth to light, create miracles of your messes, and supply all your needs. Me, not you!

We need to read Psalm 46:10 "Be still and know that I am God" in full context:

> God is our refuge and strength, an ever-present help in trouble. Therefore we will not fear, though the earth give way and the mountains fall into the heart of the sea, though its waters roar and foam and the mountains quake with their surging. There is a river whose streams make glad the city of God, the holy place where the Most High dwells. God is within her, she will not fall; God will help her at break of day. Nations are in uproar, kingdoms fall; He lifts His voice, the earth melts. The Lord Almighty is with us; the God of Jacob is our fortress. Come and see the works of the Lord, the desolations He has brought on the earth. He makes wars cease to the ends of the earth; He breaks the bow and shatters the spear, He burns

> the shields with fire. "Be still, and know that I am God; I
> will be exalted among the nations, I will be exalted in the
> earth." The LORD Almighty is with us; the God of Jacob
> is our fortress.

This is truly a powerful Scripture passage. Stop right now, be still, and let it soak in. *Selah*, a word repeated throughout the Bible, is a Hebrew term urging us to pause and think about what was said.

Ironically, Mattie has Psalm 46:10 written on her pillow from Vacation Bible School. Every evening she lays her head down on the words "Be still and know that I am God."

What do you lie your head down on at night? Late-night talk shows? Your list of homework assignments? Your worries? Your hurts? Your plans? Your dependence on others?

If you need to remind yourself, write these words on your pillow: "Be still and know that I am God." And DO be still because He is working things for good to those who know and trust Him (Rom 8:28).

Pray

Dear Heavenly Father, please forgive me for wiggling and striving and working and fretting and fussing and fighting and even forcing when I know that there are times when You have clearly told me to be still.

God, please help me to recognize there is a difference between giving up and giving up to You.

I have done all that I can do in _____ (situation, relationship, concern), and I choose today to be still and hope, trust, and delight in You.

Please help me also to take some time to be still during my busy days so I might receive your wisdom and hear your precious Holy Spirit. I love You, Lord. Amen.

Believe

Psalm 46:10 says, "Be still and know that I am God . . ."
Exodus 14:14 says, "You need only to be still."
Nehemiah 8:11 tells the people to "Be still."
Jeremiah 47:6 says to "Cease and be still."
Zechariah 2:13 says, "Be still before the Lord, all mankind."
Mark 4:39 says, "Quiet! Be still!"

Psalm 37:1–9 tells us, "Do not fret because of evil men or be envious of those who do wrong; for like the grass they will soon wither, like green plants they will soon die away. Trust in the Lord and do good; dwell in the land and enjoy safe pasture. Delight yourself in the Lord and He will give you the desires of your heart. Commit your way to the Lord; trust in Him and He will do this: He will make your righteousness shine like the dawn, the justice of your cause like the noonday sun. Be still before the Lord and wait patiently for Him; do not fret when men succeed in their ways, when they carry out their wicked schemes. Refrain from anger and turn from wrath; do not fret—it leads only to evil. For evil men will be cut off, but those who hope in the Lord will inherit the land."

Psalm 46:1–11 states, "God is our refuge and strength, an ever-present help in trouble. Therefore we will not fear, though the earth give way and the mountains fall into the heart of the sea, though its waters roar and foam and the mountains quake with their surging. There is a river whose streams make glad the city of God, the holy place where the Most High dwells. God is within her, she will not fall; God will help her at break of day. Nations are in uproar, kingdoms fall; He lifts his voice, the earth melts. The Lord Almighty is with us; the God of Jacob is our fortress. Come and see the works of the Lord, the desolations He has brought on the earth. He makes wars cease to the ends of the earth; He breaks the bow and shatters the spear, He burns the shields with fire. 'Be still, and know that I am God; I will be exalted among the nations, I will be exalted in the earth.' The Lord Almighty is with us; the God of Jacob is our fortress."

For Journaling and Reflection

1. Make a list of the things you "lay your head down on" at night. Turn that into your prayer list; give it all up to God. Write down a Scripture from this chapter that really speaks to you, then put it under your pillow when you go to bed.

2. If you've been asked by God to be still, but you just can't, what do you think is stopping you? It may be your need to stay busy to feel productive, or it may be that it's hard for you to trust God to work things out the way you'd prefer. Write a prayer asking God to give your heart peace while He works in your life.

3. Read Psalm 37:1—9, and underline all the things that are God's job. Then go back through and circle everything that's your job. Notice where you've tried to do His job in your life instead of your own. What part of your job is hardest? Easiest? What parts of God's job have you seen Him working on? What parts has He asked you to trust Him to do without your being able to see?

Twenty-two

Coveting

Appreciating Your Gifts

Exodus 20:17 says, "You shall not covet your neighbor's house. You shall not covet your neighbor's wife, or his manservant or maidservant, his ox or donkey, or anything that belongs to your neighbor."

To covet means to yearn for or desire something that you do not have or should not have. Here's a poem I wrote about coveting:

He awakened from a slumber and turned over in his bed,
as morning sun gently lighted on his sleepy head.
The birds were softly singing as he shuffled across the floor,
but nothing did he appreciate because he always wanted more.

As a youngster on Christmas mornings when he opened gifts for him,
he would peer across the room to admire gifts for "them."
Never was his heart thankful for what was intended "thine,"
since yearning for what belonged to others took up all his time.

Today he's blessed with many gifts and God has more from above,
but he may not receive them on this earth because coveting blocks
   his love.
You see, God won't give to His child that which will hurt him in the
   end,
and this sad man cannot love because the more "things" he has,
the more he covets the possessions of his friend.

Who did you think of after reading that poem? It's easy to read those words and think of other people—people who don't seem to be as grateful as they ought to be for the wonderful gifts God has given them. But take a moment and think about what God may be trying to say to *you* through this poem.

Is there something someone else has or owns that you covet right now? Maybe you wish you had your sister's iPod, or your best friend's new jeans. Maybe you wish you could go on a great beach vacation like your cousins, or that your parents would give you a brand-new car just like girl who lives next door to you.

But besides material gifts, we can also covet spiritual gifts or God-given ability gifts. This type of coveting even happens among some "mature" Christian leaders in churches. If we have a friend with a gift for offering good advice to others who have problems, we should be overjoyed that people are being cared for in such a loving way. If we have a classmate who's a brilliant speaker, and speaks out on behalf of God's heart concerning the poor and the hurting, we should rejoice that God's Word is being spread in our community. But sometimes, we feel insecure about our own gifts and abilities, and end up coveting the gifts of others.

Think about This

The Bible teaches us that we're one Body—the Body of Christ. And if we are one Body, then we should rejoice as one Body. When one part of the Body of Christ—every Christian—receives or does something well, then we should all rejoice.

Think about your physical body: Your hands don't covet your feet. Your hands don't get to wear shoes, but every day, it's your hands that help put the shoes on your feet. This is a healthy functioning body.

In her *What Is God Doing in My Life* CD series, famous Christian speaker Joyce Meyer puts it something like this: Your eyes might admire the earrings on your ears, but your eyes were not made to wear earrings. Not only would it look ridiculous for your eyes to wear earrings, it would be painful. Yet many in the Body of Christ try to wear, or do, or have, what was not meant for them simply because they covet it.

Stop and think of why the devil would want you to covet the gifts of other people. Stop and think of why God would *not* want you to covet the gifts of others.

A friend of mine is an eloquent intercessor (someone who prays constantly for others). She is close to God, and loves to spend time in conversation with Him. She prays nonstop on her knees and even forgets to eat. Not me. I can't pray nonstop on my knees for even an hour. But I can study the Bible all day (no kidding), I can write about living a Christian life, and speak for hours and hours at conferences telling others about it.

What if I coveted my friend's gift for prayer so much that I spent all my time trying to be an intercessor instead of a writer and speaker? Then I wouldn't be developing or using the gifts God has given me to glorify Him. I'd be a hand wearing a shoe or an eye wearing an earring.

Whether we covet material possessions, looks, or talents, coveting keeps us from receiving what is ours and being who we are. It keeps us from appreciating the amazing gifts that God has given us. It blocks our love. And in the end, coveting keeps us from glorifying God.

Think about This

What are your God-given gifts? Take a minute to jot down as many of your material—and spiritual—gifts as you can think of. Tack your list to your bulletin board, or tape it to the inside of your notebook. If you're ever feeling down, read over your list and tell God "Thank you!" for His amazing blessings.

Pray

Jesus, I choose this day to receive what is mine and be who You created me to be. Please forgive me for coveting _____.
Please help me to glorify You with the gifts and talents You have placed within me. I know that any good in me comes straight from You.

Please help everyone in the Body of Christ to be healed of coveting. Teach us to help each other, be excited for each other, and rejoice as one Body to the glory of Your Name. Amen.

Believe

Exodus 20:17 says, "You shall not covet your neighbor's house. You shall not covet your neighbor's wife, or his manservant or maidservant, his ox or donkey, or anything that belongs to your neighbor."

For Journaling and Reflection

1. Is there something you have a tendency to covet (clothes, electronic gadgets, circle of friends, boyfriend)? Is there a particular personality trait you have a tendency to covet (sense of humor, creativity, compassion, social skills)? Just acknowledging that you covet these things can help you be aware of a tendency and change your way of thinking.

2. What gifts of your own might you downplay or stifle because you're busy coveting other's gifts? Think of your gifts actually being put to good use. Who could benefit from them? Who is most in need of the gifts God has given you?

3. Do you know someone else who is focusing on what they don't have, rather than what they do? How can you encourage them to discover and develop their God-given gifts?

Twenty-three

Giving It All
Showing Love to Others

What does it mean to give everything we have? Here's what Jesus has to say:

> Mark 12:41–44 says, "Jesus sat down opposite the place where the offerings were put and watched the crowd putting their money into the temple treasury. Many rich people threw in large amounts. But a poor widow came and put in two very small copper coins, worth only a fraction of a penny. Calling His disciples to Him, Jesus said, 'I tell you the truth, this poor widow has put more into the treasury than all the others. They all gave out of their wealth; but she, out of her poverty, put in everything—all she had to live on.'"

Looking at other versions of the Bible can help us understand more deeply just what it means to have this kind of loving generosity:

> The Amplified Bible says, "She, out of her deep poverty, has put in everything that she had—[even] all she had on which to live."
>
> The King James Version reads, "This poor widow hath cast more in, than all they which have cast into the

> treasury; For all they did cast in of their abundance;
> but she of her want did cast in all that she had, even all
> her living."

Several years ago, I met each week with kids living at a state-run home in order to teach the Bible and to love them in the name of Jesus. The children's parents were in prison, strung out on drugs, or somehow unable to care for them.

Most of the children had been separated from their brothers and sisters, bounced from foster home to foster home, and moved from one state facility to another. An astounding number of them had been physically and emotionally abused and many of them had been members of gangs.

Every single one of those kids had experienced a life of not belonging. The result? The treasury of their little hearts had been completely bankrupted of love.

Most of us, because we've been loved by others, have a treasury of love stored up in our hearts. As children, our mothers, fathers, grandparents, brothers and sisters, friends, teachers, pastors, and others deposited love into our hearts over the years.

Even more importantly, when we chose for Jesus to be Lord of our lives, acknowledged that He is the Son of God, and asked His forgiveness, then the Holy Spirit came to live in our hearts. If we know how to receive it, the Holy Spirit constantly brings God's love into the treasury of our hearts—enough love to give out to others. The treasury of our hearts can be filled to the fullness of God's love.

> Ephesians 3:17–19 (KJV) says, "That Christ may dwell
> in your hearts by faith; that ye, being rooted and grounded
> in love, May be able to comprehend with all saints what
> is the breadth, and length, and depth, and height; And to
> know the love of Christ, which passeth knowledge, that
> ye might be filled with all the fullness of God."

The fullness of God is God's love in our hearts' treasury!

But the children I came to know at the facility had very little love deposited into their hearts. They were not only spiritually poor—they were bankrupt.

One of the ex-gang girls didn't like me at all. She told me over and over each week she didn't like me, and she didn't believe in God. Each week I dreaded seeing her, knowing she would tell me where to go and how to get there.

As funny as that sounds, I knew at least to dig into my treasury of God's overflowing love and love her, even though she had nothing in her treasury to give back to me.

Is there anyone in your life like that? Do you choose to love them out of the abundance of God's love in your heart, even though they seem to have nothing in their treasury to give back? The only way to love someone who acts "unloveable" is to love that person out of God's deposit of love in your heart without any expection of a positive reaction back from them.

Maybe someone in your grade has always ignored or belittled you. People who act emotionally bankrupt usually are. When you pass this person in the hall and give a smile and a nod even though you always receive back a scowl or indifference, God is pleased, because you are giving out HIS love stored within your heart.

God wants us to give without expecting to receive in return. And He's most honored when we give to those who can't give back. It's easy to understand this concept when it comes to material things or money. None of us would give money to a homeless person, and then hold out our hands in order to receive something in return.

In the same way, none of us would write to the Red Cross or the local food bank and say, "I gave a turkey, three cans of food, and all my babysitting money to the Jones family through your organization. And I'm still waiting for the Jones family to give me a turkey dinner and cash in return."

We think those examples of material expectations from those who have nothing to give in return are ridiculous. But if we're honest, many of us do this to people in a spiritual sense.

All of us, at one time or another, make the mistake of expecting love from somebody who just can't give it. "Look!" we might think. "I've been nice, reached out, said kind things, and been loving. And what do I get in return? Nothing! Absolutely nothing!" Or maybe in return for kindness you've received rudeness or worse.

Back to my little story: Each week that determined young woman told me she didn't like me and didn't believe in God. And each week, I returned with God's love—not my own—and gave her some out of the treasury He had placed in my heart.

God does a strange thing when we're willing to give out of our treasury. The more love we give away, the more love we get back in return. It's the direct opposite of natural law, which says the more you give, then the less you have. But giving out of God's treasury has nothing to do with natural law; it's all about spiritual law.

> ### Think about This
>
> God's spiritual law: "The more you give, the more you receive."

Here's how the Bible puts it: "Give, and it will be given to you. A good measure, pressed down, shaken together and running over, will be poured into your lap. For with the measure you use, it will be measured to you" (Luke 6:38).

So every time I gave to this young girl, God made sure somehow I got refilled with even more love, either straight from Him (usually when reading His refreshing, heart-filling Word) or from other people (extra kindnesses and favors that I knew God had set up).

After a few months, this young woman walked up to me when I entered the facility. I braced myself expecting to hear the usual threats and obscenities, but she said something different: "Hey man, I believe in God . . . and you're okay." She jammed fists into her pockets while rocking from foot to foot.

"What made you say that?" I stammered.

"Well, you wouldn't leave your nice house and your nice neighborhood and your nice family, and drive all the way up here week after week after week to tell us about nothin'."

I was so excited that she finally saw the love of God and believed in Him! But I also learned an important lesson: Love keeps giving without expecting to receive, because it's in the giving of love that others see Truth—they see God—and love is increased.

And it's in the receiving of love that spiritually bankrupt people can finally love.

Just like the widow in the Gospel of Mark, this young girl gave me the treasure of her heart. Although small, she gave me approval and love out of her poverty and her own desire for approval and love.

What do you have in the treasury of your heart? Have many people have given love to you over the years, making your heart full of love? Has God deposited love into your treasury, and you are now overflowing and rich? Or do you have hardships and circumstances in your life that have emptied the treasury of your heart?

Jesus is sitting by the temple treasury just as He was in Mark's Gospel. He's watching and waiting. He's not asking us to give the same amount that anybody else is giving. But rich or poor—no matter how much we've got—He wants us to give it all.

Prayer

Dear Jesus, please forgive me from withholding love from You and from others. Please forgive me for loving others in my life, especially family and friends, with the expectation of getting love in return. I trust You that when I give, You'll see to it that my treasury of love is filled even more. Please give me the grace to love spiritually bankrupt people even if they insult me and make me feel foolish. Please help me to recognize when spiritually bankrupt people are just doing the best they can. Please help me never to judge others, but to continually ask for Your grace to love no matter what. Amen.

Believe

"Jesus sat down opposite the place where the offerings were put and watched the crowd putting their money into the temple treasury. Many rich people threw in large amounts. But a poor widow came and put in two very small copper coins, worth only a fraction of a penny. Calling His disciples to Him, Jesus said, 'I tell you the truth, this poor widow has put more into the treasury than all the others. They all gave out of their wealth; but she, out of her poverty, put in everything—all she had to live on'" (Mark 12:41–44).

"Give, and it will be given to you. A good measure, pressed down, shaken together and running over, will be poured into your lap. For with the measure you use, it will be measured to you" (Luke 6:38).

For Journaling and Reflection

1. Have you ever gone out of your way to be nice to someone who was cruel or rude to you in return? Did their reaction affect the way you behaved the next opportunity you had to be nice to them? Can seeing that person as someone who may not have much to give make it a little easier to love them with God's love anyway?

2. Think of how your life would have to look in order to treat someone the way the spiritually bankrupt treat others. What type of unbearable pain or sadness must that person have to endure? Does that make it easier not expect anything in return? Ask God to see them through his eyes, then pray for them from that perspective.

Twenty-four

God Keeps His Promises
Applying Scripture to Your Life

This last chapter in *Dare to Be Rare* is a little different from the rest. I want to leave you with a treasury of God's Word—Scriptures that you can apply to situations for the rest of your lives. So I want us to read and reflect together.

As I was praying recently, I heard in my heart: "God keeps His promises." Of course, I thought, we *know* God keeps promises because God always tells the truth. But I heard it again: "God keeps His promises." So I looked up the word "keeps."

"Keeps" means "reserves, maintains, supports, celebrates, detains, sets aside, sustains, holds, preserves, and keeps safe."

What I didn't expect to hear was the Holy Spirit whisper, "My children *are* my promises." In other words, God keeps (reserves, maintains, supports, celebrates, detains, sets aside, sustains, holds, preserves, and keeps safe) *us!*

Stop here and grab your journal, or find some space at the end of this chapter. Write down one meaning of "keep" that you've experienced in your life from the definition you've just read. When and how has God reserved, maintained, supported, celebrated, detained, set aside, sustained, held, or preserved you? Then get ready to share.

Okay, I'll go first. I've learned that because I'm God's promise, He will *keep* me by *detaining* me. I tend to go full speed ahead whenever God points me in a certain direction, so most any kind of detainment is hard for me.

For example, after Lacey and I had been married for several years, God began to point our hearts in the direction of aiding the spiritual and practical needs of orphans living in poor nations. At the same time, I began working with American high school youth, many of whom seemed to have everything but a sense of purpose or a conviction that they were making a difference.

Since we had always been drawn to Russia and the Baltic region, it made sense that we plan a mission trip for my American students to go with us to supply, teach, help build, and share the gospel.

Once my husband and I decided to go for it, I spent every free minute planning the mission trip—from travel schedules to student release forms, from trip insurance to translators. Finally it was time to ask our home church if they'd be willing to support us financially.

I remember well the morning we were to make our appeal at our church's evening mission meeting. Lacey came downstairs for breakfast and said, "You know, I just don't have a sense of peace about our going to Russia anymore."

I said, "What do you mean?"

"Well, I *did* have a feeling of peace about it until yesterday, but now when I think about going, I'm uncomfortable."

"Oh," I poured cereal into my bowl and passed it to him, "it must be that you're concerned about missing work."

"No," he shook his head, "that's not it."

"Then is it the political unrest there?"

"No."

"Feel funny about asking the church for money?"

"Not it."

"Then what is it?" I asked, putting my spoon down and tilting my head to one side.

"I don't know exactly. But my sense of peace about the whole mission trip is gone. I think we should call the church and tell them that we aren't going. And let the students know too."

I lost my appetite. My husband is never domineering or unreasonable. After several years of marriage, we'd learned to respect one another's feelings and intuitions. I could tell that he felt strongly about this, so I decided to go along with his change of mind—even though I wanted to go now. Why didn't Lacey have faith for the trip like I did?

I was frustrated by God's detainment through my husband's lack of peace. Over the next several weeks I thought about all my hard work and what it would've been like to go.

The more I thought about it, the more frustrated and grumpy I became, especially in the morning—almost to the point of nausea. I began to feel more and more nauseous, morning after morning.

You guessed it. We found out we were expecting! And if we'd gone to Russia, I would have been nauseous and two months pregnant in a foreign country where we couldn't drink the water or understand the language, where we would have been in charge of directing a dozen or more teenagers every minute of every day.

God keeps us sometimes by *detaining* us—making us wait or even stop—so that He can protect us and fulfill a greater purpose. Seven months later, Matlin Kathleen, the baby that many doctors believed I would never have because of my total spinal fusion as a result of scoliosis, was born in San Antonio, Texas.

But seven years later our family reached even beyond Russia to the small nation of Armenia to adopt our son, Storm Jameson. And God, perhaps as sign of His faithfulness to me, gave our children a small birthmark in the same place on their legs.

That's one of my many family stories about God *keeping* us. God will always keep His promises (us), even when we are not keeping our promises, even when we are not faithful to Him.

God says even when we are not faithful, He remains faithful to us—His promises. "If we are faithless, He will remain faithful, for He cannot disown Himself" (2 Tim 2:13).

As a matter of fact, God says He will remain faithful to us forever. Psalm 146:5–6 says, "Blessed is He whose help is the God of Jacob, whose hope is in the LORD his God, the Maker of heaven and earth, the sea, and everything in them—the LORD, who remains faithful forever."

God placed the following Scriptures on my heart for you. Read and ponder each one.

> "And my God will meet all your needs according to His glorious riches in Christ Jesus. To our God and Father be glory for ever and ever. Amen." (Phil 4:19–20)

What does the above Scripture say about the One Who is keeping you?

How does this promise apply personally to you right now?

> "Trust in the LORD with all your heart and lean not on your own understanding; in all your ways acknowledge Him, and He will make your paths straight. Do not be wise in your own eyes; fear the LORD and shun evil. This will bring health to your body and nourishment to your bones. Honor the LORD with your wealth, with the first fruits of all your crops; then your barns will be filled to overflowing, and your vats will brim over with new wine." (Prov 3:5–10)

What does the above Scripture say about the One Who is keeping you?

How does this promise apply personally to you right now?

> "Rejoice in the Lord always. I will say it again: Rejoice! Let your gentleness be evident to all. The Lord is near. Do not be anxious about anything, but in everything, by prayer and petition, with thanksgiving, present your requests to God. And the peace of God, which transcends all understanding, will guard your hearts and your minds in Christ Jesus. Finally, brothers, whatever is true, whatever is noble, whatever is right, whatever is pure, whatever is lovely, whatever is admirable—if anything is excellent or praiseworthy—think about such things." (Phil 4:4–8)

What does the above Scripture say about the One Who is keeping you?

How does this promise apply personally to you right now?

> "They cried to you and were saved; in you they trusted
> and were not disappointed." (Ps 22:5)

What does the above Scripture say about the One Who is keeping you?

How does this promise apply personally to you right now?

> "As the Scripture says, 'Anyone who trusts in Him will
> never be put to shame [or disappointed].'" (Rom 10:11)

What does the above Scripture say about the One Who is keeping you?

How does this promise apply personally to you right now?

> "For He will command His angels concerning you to
> keep you in all your ways." (Ps 91:11)

What does the above Scripture say about the One Who is keeping you?

How does this promise apply personally to you right now?

Right now, what big things in your life do you need to trust to God, Who always keeps His promises? List them:

What little things do you need to put in God's hands so that He may take care of them? List them:

Add to the above list as big and small concerns come to you during the day. Rereading and meditating on the Scriptures in this chapter allows the Holy Spirit to convince (which is a Greek synonym for "convict") you that *God keeps His promises.* God keeps *YOU!* And when you have faith for that "all things are possible!" (Luke 1:37a).

Prayer

Write your own prayer here.

Believe

In your own words, rewrite the Scripture passages from this chapter—or from other chapters in the book—that mean the most to you right now.

Appendix
Dare to Be Rare 2007

One hundred and eight-five girls attended, forty-four girls requested that the *kathleen whitten ministries* **Prayer Team** contact them for follow-up prayer, and girls girls asked Jesus to be their Lord and Savior for the very first time! A big thanks to parent volunteers and "Chapter 3" band.

At the end of the evening, all the girls were given a questionnaire to fill out. Below are a few comments *kwm* has permission from the girls to share.

We adults have much to learn from their openness, humility, honesty, ability to learn (especially from peers), and willingness to "Dare to Be Rare" for God!

Our words cannot begin to describe Dare to Be Rare 2007, so let's read what the girls had to say.

DTBR 2007 Girl Comments

Some ways the world tells me that "I am not good enough" are:
"Not pretty enough; never had a boyfriend—lack of acceptance." (12th grader); "Movie stars, TV, magazines." (8th grader); "Just walking down the halls of school you feel inferior, not cool, good, pretty, smart enough." (12th grader); "Getting kicked out of a group." (6th grader); "The way I look. . . . I am always self-conscious about my weight." (12th grader); "Magazines, TV shows, and models." (8th grader); "Grades." (10th grader); "Not being as smart as most of my friends." (7th grader); "Not having a boyfriend." (8th grader); "Not tall enough to model." (9th grader); "I don't get invited to things and feel left out." (8th grader); "My body is not . . ." (9th grader); "Peer pressure." (9th grader); "You have to be

skinny." (9th grader); "Not popular enough" (6th grader); "Not accepted the way I am." (7th grader); "Not important like other girls." (6th grader); "How much money you have and if you are perfect or not." (8th grader); "They talk in front of me about plans [I am not included in]." (6th grader); "TV shows like 'NEXT.'" (8th grader); "That I am not worth anything." (8th grader); "A nickname . . . that really hurts." (6th grader); "Being purposely ignored." (6th grader); "Not sporty" (6th grader); "That I can't do anything right." (11th grader); "Not being stupid enough . . . since guys don't like really smart girls." (9th grader); "Comparisons." (9th grader); "People yelling at me." (6th grader); "Feeling very insignificant." (10th grader); "When I make a mistake at volleyball practice." (9th grader); "When people don't listen to me." (12th grader); "My body . . . no matter what my [sport-teacher] says." (9th grader); "People not liking me back." (12th grader); "Not talented enough." (9th grader); "It's hard to think of what I am good at." (10th grader); "The way I look." (6th grader); "Told I'm not 'girly' enough." (12th grader); "My skin isn't clear." (11th grader); "Not having the right clothes." (10th grader); "When girls talk about me." (6th grader); "Cliques" (9th grader); "My mom says I'm too big for my size . . . parents bug me about grades . . . living up to my little sister . . . not being in the in-crowd." (9th grade); "When I lose a tennis match." (9th grader); "Being made fun of." (7th grader); "I don't fit the right 'image' of what a girl is supposed to wear/act." (9th grader); "I'm weird, ugly." (7th grader); "Not rich" (8th grade); "Celebrities" (10th grader); "When people laugh at you." (7th grader); "I don't have the 'in-style' clothes." (10th grader); "That I don't drink." (9th grader).

Some things the Dare to Be Rare girl leaders "dared" that spoke directly to me are:
"About not falling into temptation and to be yourself and your true friends will accept you for that." (8th grader); "Step out of my box and reach out to people other than myself, love one another more than myself." (10th grader); "Because your husband is out there somewhere, he wants you to stay pure." (12th grader); "That the most important thing you can do [in life] is to follow God." (7th grader); "To be patient that God will provide me with a soul mate just for me." (8th grader); "Listen to God to hear His perfect plan for me." (8th grader); "That my husband is out there right now." (7th grader); "To be your true self and you will be rewarded."

(8th grader); "Treat your body as a temple and don't be anxious." (7th grader); "Not procrastinate, pray more." (7th grader); "Not being anxious." (7th grader); "A man will love me some day, just the way that God made me." (9th grader); "Be grateful for what I have." (10th grader); "Dare to go into the world, trusting Christ. Be yourself and help others to be themselves." (9th grader); "Not being anxious, waiting for my husband, loving and trusting God before a [serious] relationship." (6th grader); "Being a friend to God." (9th grader); "Listen to God. Be yourself." (6th grader); "Purity." (9th grader); "Not to be anxious because God does have a plan just for you." (6th grader); "That you can like yourself even if your sibling is smarter." (9th grader); "To follow God's path for you even if it is not what you had planned because His way is always best." (9th grader); "Not being anxious and following Jesus. Everything that's supposed to happen will, at the perfect time, I need to be patient and faithful." (10th grader); "Your body is a temple." (9th grader); "Keeping no record of wrongs; being Christ-like each day." (12th grader); "About enjoying your life now with what you have and not putting off accepting God." (11th grader); "When they [all] talked about [how] God has a path and purpose for you." (11th grader); "Keep my faith in Christ strong and not fade out." (11th grader); "Stepping out of your comfort zone." (9th grader); "Listening to God." (9th grader); "When they all dared us to be ourselves." (9th grader).

Some things Kathleen said about herself and her life that meant a lot to me are:
"The stress she put on loving moms. I need to be more open and really show my need and devotion to [my mom]." (12th grader); "Everything she said got put in my ear and it will stay forever." (6th grader); "Her ability to be real with her stories and life" (12th grader); "The fact that she lived through cancer and learned so many wonderful things!" (8th grader); "We can all relate with her stories . . . of her struggles through junior high and high school. I like to hear about how her friends, family, and faith got her through." (10th grader); "She told us how to handle hard decisions as they come along." (7th grader); "Not letting pain take over her life." (12th grader); "When she speaks to me, I feel better about myself." (11th grader); "She leads me closer to God and brings Him into my life even more." (9th grader); "How God might use our hard times [now] to some day witness to another group of girls like us." (10th grader); "[Now] I feel

closer to my sibling." (6th grader); "Not to listen to the world because I am special and important!" (6th grader); "This has changed my life!" (6th grader); "Everyone is beautiful in their own way." (6th grader); "That being kind to people comes back around." (9th grader); "That moms are girls and to love yourself." (6th grader); "When she said that people need people; we need people and told the story of receiving blood transfusions and when she talked about our mothers and how much they love us." (9th grader); "That God can heal your mind." (9th grader); "Being vulnerable and forgiving again and again." (12th grader); "You just blew my mind away when you talked to us! It made me feel like I was really beautiful on the inside. And you made me know that I should just be myself because God made me that way and [we all] like you for that. Thank you for speaking to ME!" (6th grader).

To me, "Dare to Be Rare" means:
"Living my life outside my comfort zone and declaring my love for God daily through actions no matter what others think." (12th grader); "Being myself . . . the true Christ-like me." (12th grader); "Reach out to others who are less fortunate. Take charge in your life and follow Jesus." (10th grader); "Being unique and outstanding—a light in the darkness." (12th grader); "Dare to be a soldier for God. Representing Him." (12th grader); "To be the girl who shines through for Jesus even though I might be the only one." (10th grader); "Don't try to be someone you're not." (11th grader); "Having your actions show God's love." (10th grader); "Getting to know myself and God better." (9th grader); "Be yourself. Do what God tells you to do. Spread the Word. It's the only thing that matters." (8th grader); "That everyone is special in God's eyes." (6th grader); "Going out of your 'safe' boundaries." (8th grader); "Rebelling against who the world says you should be." (12th grader); "Embrace [the real] you!" (9th grader); "To be your complete self." (6th grader); "Appreciating who you are." (9th grader); "Dare to Be Different" (7th grader); "Be different than everyone else by following Jesus and not the way of the world." (9th grader); "To live for God in a world that is not living for Him." (12th grader); "Don't conform to the world to be accepted even if that means not being 'pretty' enough or not having a boyfriend." (10th grader); "Be myself and not conform to the pattern of this world. I am beautiful just the way I am." (12th grader); "God has created each of us to be rare!" (12th grader); "Not be

ashamed or embarrassed to be a Christian and who God made me [to be]." (12th grader); "Realizing that we are just the way God wanted us to be and that we have to be rare to be able to fulfill the purpose He has given us." (12th grader); "To not conform to what people tell you, you should be and to be true to yourself to be truly happy." (11th grader); "Go against the crowd when you know what they are doing is wrong and don't be afraid to stick up for what you believe in." (8th grader); "A place where girls can just be girls not worrying about people judging us." (8th grader); "To be a sister in Christ; to be an 'i' on the cross." (10th grader); "Take a chance, be yourself—not who others want you to be." (9th grader); "Jesus accepted His 'dare' and died for us." (9th grader); "Do not conform to the world's view, but conform to God's idea of a woman." (11th grader); "Don't conform. Transform. Renew your mind so you can be all that God created you to be. DTBR 2007. Romans 12:2." (9th grader).

Because of Dare to Be Rare 2007, I dare to:
"Forgive and love everybody; to be Christ to everybody I can." (12th grader); "Love [others] with every inch of my body, soul, and spirit and I pray that others change their ways [too] through this awesome experience." (10th grader); "Be myself and no one else." (6th grader); "Fix a lot of things in my life that I know I've needed to but haven't had the courage and strength to do." (12th grader); "Put my faith first." (12th grader); "Live through Christ and show others the way." (10th grader); "Not put God on the back burner." (10th grader); "Not compare myself to others." (9th grader); "Be a closer follower of Christ." (9th grader); "Become closer to God." (8th grader); "Be a huge light for Christ! (10th grader); "Not run away." (8th grader); "Be myself and no one else!" (8th grader); "Be myself and trust in God!" (6th grader); "Put God first." (8th grader); "Be open with God. Not be afraid to talk with Him and others about how I really feel." (9th grader); "Be the best [her name] I can be!" (6th grader); "Be special, but not exclusive." (7th grader); "Stop trying to impress people and just be who God wants me to be." (10th grader); "Lead my own path." (7th grader); "Be myself completely and love others for who they really are." (12th grader); "Be patient and wait because God does everything for a reason and have faith in His choices." (10th grader); "I dare to be confident with God!" (6th grader); "Stop trying to please everyone and let my true self show." (9th grader); "Live life now—don't worry about

what others think. Be you—all of you!" (9th grader); "Be pure and be less of me and more of God." (12th grader); "Not be ashamed." (9th grader); "Forgive myself." (12th grader); "To live." (11th grader); "Seek God before anything else." (12th grader); "Show others Christ without preaching." (10th grader); "Know that God created me beautifully in His image and I am beautiful and unique in my own way." (10th grader); "Not let other people bring me down." (9th grader); "Not give up!" (12th grader).

Tonight I asked Jesus to come into my heart for the first time:
"I sat up crying and knowing that I was a new person!" (9th grader); "And I feel so cleansed." (8th grader); "I have done things that need to be forgiven and I really need Jesus to direct me in the right way." (6th grader); "I felt a warmth, a comfort, knowing what He [Jesus] did [for me on the cross]. And that God is there to listen to me." (9th grader); "One of the team leaders said [to] let God into your life so I did by asking Him to forgive me for all of my sins." (6th grader); "It felt so nice and great!" (6th grader); "[I felt Him] Jesus come into my heart!" (7th grader); "Very emotional" (9th grader); "I asked for forgiveness and for His help!" (9th grader); "It felt good. I know [now] that I have someone when I think I don't. I can feel great!" (8th grader); "And I felt like a shining star and that I could finally talk to my mom." (6th grader); "I never really understood how to ask Jesus into my heart until tonight." (8th grader).

Tonight (through Jesus) I asked God for forgiveness and forgave myself for:
"For being too hard on my mother and father and for the problems they face and the extra pressure I put on them." (9th grader); "Being jealous and for being mad and caring too much on how I look." (6th grader); "Being mean to people who deserve to be treated well." (7th grader); "Sometimes thinking that I am superior to others and I'm not." (9th grader); "Putting up a façade; not practicing what I preach." (10th grader); "Putting myself in a bad relationship and disrespecting myself." (7th grader); "Fighting with my family, being rude to people, and talking behind their backs." (9th grader); "Allowing myself to get wrapped up into the darkness of the world." (9th grader); "Not making good choices." (7th grader); "Not always being me." (6th grader); "Judging others." (8th grader); "Thinking bad things about myself." (6th grader); "Selfishness" (9th grader); "Very bad

choices." (11th grader); "Starting rumors." (6th grader); "Rejecting myself." (12th grader); "Thinking that I was okay to treat my sister the way I have been." (9th grader); "Doing many bad things that made me try to fit in with others. . . . It really brought me lower." (10th grader); "Not being the sacred temple I should be for God." (12th grader); "Hating who I was before I let Christ back into my life and consciously into my heart again." (12th grader); "Bad social decisions." (11th grader); "Being impatient and ungrateful toward my parents." (11th grader); "For being bad to my mom." (6th grader); "Making really bad decisions that I regret." (11th grader); "An unkind act I committed against myself and others." (8th grader); "Being rude and disagreeable on purpose to my parents." (8th grader); "Breaking my [own] heart." (12th grader).

Tonight I asked forgiveness from others for:
"Judging and jumping to conclusions—I am going to be more accepting" (12th grader); "Being mean and exclusive to a girl [last year]" (8th grader); "Acting like I was too good for them." "Being judgmental." (9th grader); "Gossiping." (8th grader); "Being disrespectful." (9th grader); "Being rude to a friend" (8th grader); "I had a rocky year with one of the girls here and asked for forgiveness and we are closer now." (8th grader); "Hurting them emotionally since I never truly asked for forgiveness before." (8th grader); "Thinking some [girls] were more important than others." (6th grader); "Holding grudges." (9th grader); "Gossiping" (8th grader); "My mom. I love her so much. I just asked for forgiveness for anytime I've been short-tempered with her, or simply mean." (9th grader); "Being mean and gossiping. Sorry!" (6th grader); "Being bossy to my family and sister." (7th grader); "Being mean and having a fight. Because of DTBR, I am back together with [a good friend]!" (6th grader); "Distancing myself from [friends]—not reaching out." (12th grader); "Telling secrets that [others] had trusted me with." (11th grader); "Being mad at my father." (11th grader); "Being mean to [friends] and starting off on the 'wrong foot.'" (9th grader); "Losing touch; hurting someone I love; disappointing my family." (7th grader).

I want to tell Kathleen:
"Dare to Be Rare has really put me really close to God." (6th grader); "That I feel so great after this! My mom is always telling me that I need

a Christ-centered life and you have really motivated me to do so." (7th grader); "You are one of my biggest role models and I love you." (12th grader); "Thank you for being such an amazing leader!" (12th grader); "Thank you for Dare to Be Rare. It's a cool experience! You are a brave person!" (8th grader); "I appreciate your love toward the girls. I look at 'love' in a totally different way now." (12th grader); "Dare is so much more than I expected! Thank you for all the time and effort." (11th grader); "That DTBR was a wonderful idea because it helps girls to love themselves for who they really are." (9th grader); "You have been through so much and I look up to you because you turned to God every time." (10th grader); "Thank you for changing my life for the better." (9th grader); "She is great at helping others to know the Lord better." (6th grader); "That she helped open my eyes toward God's [love for me]. I always thought I knew God, I did, but not like I do now! And I am so thankful for that! I am so glad to come to this amazing experience!" (8th grader); "Thank you for being so positive all the time and telling me how great God is!" (9th grader); "That I am grateful that she has taken time out of her life to change my life." (9th grader); "That you went through so much, but you are still loving and giving and want to tell the world about God." (8th grader); "That she has inspired me to be myself." (6th grader); "That you make me open my eyes and see things about Jesus that I would never have seen." (10th grader); "That we all relate to you! Can you speak to us again?" (9th grader); "You made me realize that I need to love myself too [as you do]." (12th grader); "You are my hero!" (12th grader); "I left [forever] changed." (10th grader); "By listening to what she has to say, I have made new decisions in my life." (10th grader); "And you have impacted my life so much!" (12th grader); "I'm really proud of her." (9th grader); "You are my guiding light to God!" (12th grader); "That DTBR has touched me and helped me understand more about God. And I want to thank her because I already feel different and closer to God." (8th grader); "I respect everything she says and love listening to her speak." (9th grader); "That she is a wonderful example of a Christian walking with Christ." (10th grader); "That she is an inspiration who has pointed my heart in the right direction." (10th grader); "That she has powerful wisdom that I look up to and I know a lot of others do too." (9th grader); "I love you Mommy! You're the best Mommy in the world!" (6th grader).

Kathleen's Message to DTBR Girls:

I am so proud of each of you and I love you. You opened your heart to listen, your mind to change, and your spirit to Dare to Be Rare. So I continue to dare you to rebel against the world by seeking God in every area of your life, loving the people around you, and being yourself and no one else.

Kathleen's Message to DTBR Jr./Sr. Leaders:

It was an honor to meet with you for the month prior to Dare. In such a short time all sixteen of you grew and changed! You did an amazing job during DTBR. Your willingness to share your lives and faith in Jesus so honestly made an eternal difference in the lives of so many! I love you.